D1284637

THE CADEN CHRONICLES
RUMOR OF A
WEREWOLF

EDDIE JONES

illuminateYA
f i c t i o n

Nobles County Library
407 12th Street
Worthington, MN 56187
31315002344062

RUMOR OF A WEREWOLF BY EDDIE JONES
Published by Illuminate YA
An imprint of Lighthouse Publishing of the Carolinas
2333 Barton Oaks Dr., Raleigh, NC, 27614

ISBN: 9781645262336
Copyright © 2019 by Eddie Jones
Cover design by Elaina Lee
Illustration by: Nadezhda Tarmina
Interior design by AtriTeX Technologies P Ltd

Available in print from your local bookstore, online, or from the publisher at: ShopLPC.com

For more information on this book and the author visit: edddiejones.org

All rights reserved. Non-commercial interests may reproduce portions of this book without the express written permission of Lighthouse Publishing of the Carolinas, provided the text does not exceed 500 words. When reproducing text from this book, include the following credit line: *"Rumor of a Werewolf* by Eddie Jones published by Lighthouse Publishing of the Carolinas. Used by permission."

Commercial interests: No part of this publication may be reproduced in any form, stored in a retrieval system, or transmitted in any form by any means—electronic, photocopy, recording, or otherwise—without prior written permission of the publisher, except as provided by the United States of America copyright law.

This is a work of fiction. Names, characters, and incidents are all products of the author's imagination or are used for fictional purposes. Any mentioned brand names, places, and trademarks remain the property of their respective owners, bear no association with the author or the publisher, and are used for fictional purposes only.

Scripture quotation (Daniel 4:13–7, 33) taken from the Holy Bible, New International Version®, NIV®. Copyright ©1973, 1978, 1984, 2011 by Biblica, Inc.™. Used by permission of Zondervan. All rights reserved worldwide. www.zondervan.com. "NIV" and "New International Version" are trademarks registered in the United States Patent and Trademark Office by Biblica, Inc.™

Library of Congress Cataloging-in-Publication Data
Jones, Eddie
Rumor of a Werewolf / Eddie Jones 1st ed.

Printed in the United States of America

TABLE OF CONTENTS

CHAPTER

1

Rumor of a Werewolf

A loud, violent gust blew off the Atlantic, full of Arctic chill. Though we were only a few days away from Thanksgiving, Savannah, Georgia, felt like Kansas in January. If you've never been to Kansas in January, you haven't missed much.

I'm from Kansas and I don't miss it at all.

The screaming blast of salt-laden air caused the old trawler to shift and creak and groan. Beneath the floorboards the boat's bilge pump kicked on and a gurgling sound started. The boat's bilge pump ran a lot.

Like, all the time. Like, when I'd get up at night to go use the *head* (fancy boat term for bathroom), the bilge pump would be running. And it would still be running when I drifted off to sleep. And woke up in the morning. And went to bed at night.

I'm pretty sure the bilge pump was the only thing keeping the trawler from sinking.

When you hear the word *trawler*, you might think of a shrimp boat with lots of nets and booms. But it turns out *trawler* means big fancy luxury yacht.

Except there was nothing comfortable or luxurious about the one we had been staying on. And now we had to vacate.

"Seriously? Uncle Phil is making us leave?" I said.

"Not Phil. The owner," Dad said. "He sold the boat. We need to get off so it can be surveyed. I'm flying out tomorrow to help your mother pack. We'll drive the rental truck back sometime next week."

"What about me?"

"I'm shipping you north to Izzy's."

"Who's Izzy?"

"Isabel Canon. You know, your mom's childhood best friend? Your mom talks about her all the time."

"No, Dad, that's you."

I had a hunch Mom resented the fact that Dad and this Izzy person hit it off so well at my parents' wedding. I wasn't there, obviously. But I hear things. Sometimes the things I hear involve my parents using loud voices.

"Can't I fly back and help you and Mom pack?"

"That's two plane tickets. We can't even afford mine."

Dad had a point. He was the only one drawing a paycheck, and since he was working on straight commission at the real estate company, it was hardly a paycheck at all.

"Besides, you'd have to go through security. We can't risk that."

"Maybe we're overreacting. Could be he's not even out there looking for me."

"You want to take that chance? Anyway, there won't be any room for you in the rental truck."

I should back up and explain some things.

A few weeks back, a zombie took Wendy. Wendy is my sister, unfortunately. Clearly it wasn't a real zombie. There are no such things as zombies even though there are like a gazillion zombie shows and movies. I helped the police find my sister, but in doing so the crazy zombie kidnapper grabbed me, staked me to an oyster bed, and drowned me.

Except not really.

I held my breath for over two minutes, then escaped. But the guy who tried to kill me got away. We think he thinks I'm dead. My death was reported in the local news. I wrote my own obituary. Had fun with that. Anyway, since then I've pretty much camped out here at the marina and gone around wearing a too-large blue boat yard maintenance jump suit for a guy named *Hank*. Apparently Hank was not fond of bathing or doing laundry.

"She has a daughter," Dad said.

"Who?"

"Izzy. Should be close to your age. Your mother and Izzy were expecting at the same time."

I never told my sister Wendy this, but secretly I think Mom wishes she'd married up and into money like her childhood best friend. Dad tries hard, but we never have been what you call rich. Or even well-off. Mostly we make do.

Sometimes we don't even make that.

"It's only for a few days. Just long enough for your mother and I to get packed up and drive back here. Maybe if you have time you can visit your grandfather."

Dad meant Mom's father who has always been one of my favorite relatives. Except Pop doesn't remember things too well and one of the things he doesn't remember is that I'm his grandson.

"We're moving into a small rental apartment when we get back. It's not big, but at least it doesn't leak like this boat." Dad pulled a smudged newspaper clipping out of his shirt pocket. "Izzy thought you might find this article interesting." He passed it over to me.

Izzy. Dad was definitely giving off vibes that he still had a thing for Mom's friend.

"The *Daily Crawler?* Seriously, a newspaper?"

"Not everyone gets their news off the Internet."

I began reading.

September 30: Sleepy Hollow, New York, *The Daily Crawler*

Horrified law enforcement officials investigating the gruesome death of Candee Brenneman claim a wolf or some other large animal killed her. Brenneman, age 32, an avid jogger and fitness instructor, was found by an employee of RIP's Restaurant under a bridge in Rockefeller State Park. Brenneman's throat was savagely ripped apart. Large misshapen paw prints were found around the body. There were also bite marks on her hands and arms. Some have suggested that her death, occurring during a full moon, indicates that a werewolf may be running loose in Sleepy Hollow. The investigation is ongoing.

"Izzy knows how much you love a good mystery," Dad said.

"How could she possibly know that?"

"Your mother told her about the murder you solved in that ghost town in Deadwood Canyon."

"Was it Mom or you?"

Dad took the clipping back from me. "Do me a favor, Nick. Try to stay out of trouble. I don't want to get a call from Sleepy Hollow telling me you've been picked up for interfering in a police investigation."

Which of course was Dad's way of saying: *Don't embarrass me in front of Izzy.*

"I'll try, Dad."

"I know you will. I'm only asking you to try extra hard this time."

Because (and Dad didn't say this, but I knew he was thinking it) *I don't want you embarrassing me in front of Izzy.*

Sometimes being the grown-up in a father-son relationship is hard work.

An hour later, Uncle Phil let me out at the Amtrak station in Savannah.

"Sorry Kat couldn't come to see you off," he said.

"No worries. It's not like Lynchburg is right around the corner." I stood beside the car, holding the door open. "How is she, by the way?"

"You'd hardly recognize her. She's cut her hair and gotten rid of that ball cap she wore all the time. She looks more and more like my sister every time I see her." Uncle Phil got a serious look on his face. "Kat misses you, Nick."

"Did she tell you that?"

"No, but I can tell."

I swallowed. Then I swallowed again. Kat was a friend girl but not *my girlfriend*, if you know what I mean. "Keep an eye on that Catalina in slip twenty-nine. The bilge pump has been acting up. Runs nonstop, sometimes even when the bilge is empty."

Uncle Phil nodded. "I'll check ever' so often."

"And the forward hatch on the Pearson still leaks. I moved the cushions so they wouldn't get wet, but if it's going out on a charter, you'll need to mop up first."

"I'll make sure nothing sinks while you're gone." He leaned over and handed me a sticky note. "That's Kat's new mailing address. I'm sure she'd love a postcard from wherever you're going. Now you better go catch your train."

I tucked Kat's address into my back pocket and slammed the door shut.

Minutes later, I settled into a coach seat in the first passenger car behind the locomotive. The side-to-side rocking of the car had the comfortable feel of the trawler, making me drowsy.

Gazing out my window, I worried what I'd find in Sleepy Hollow. Not a werewolf. There's no such thing.

But there was one time, a long time ago, when this really rich and powerful king got turned into a "wolf man." At least that's what my grandfather used to tell me. So maybe me going to stay with Mom's childhood best friend wasn't the worst idea in the world.

CHAPTER

2

Grumpy in Sleepy Hollow

The desk clerk at the Headless Horseman studied me over rimless reading glasses and sighed. "Young man, there simply is no way you can leave your luggage with us unless you are a guest. Our policy is clearly posted." In case I was blind, he thumped the sheet of rules that was taped to the counter.

"I understand. What I'm asking is for you to make an exception. I need to go visit my grandfather, and he lives in a nursing home a few blocks from here."

The desk clerk straightened to his full height and glared down at me. "What you are suggesting is simply out of the question. I cannot possibly allow you to clutter our lobby with your luggage."

The lobby was a small parlor the size of an airport body scanner. So in a way, Grumpy had a point. He and Dad would have probably gotten along like best buds.

"How much?"

"The amount is hardly the issue."

"It's only for a few hours," I said.

He sighed. Sighing seemed to be his default answer to everything. "Twenty dollars."

"For one duffle bag and a daypack?"

"Per piece."

More guests were entering the lobby. They did not appear to be your typical B&B guests. There was a man dressed in a Sherlock Holmes outfit (plaid hat with ear-flaps, along with a matching cape, pipe, and magnifying glass). Beside him stood a woman who resembled Jessica Fletcher from *Murder, She Wrote*.

I placed two twenty-dollar bills on the counter. If Dad had known I was even considering spending that kind of money to let some desk clerk keep an eye on my stuff, he would have blown an artery. But the thing was, I'd already hauled my things all the way from the train station and I wasn't keen on the idea of lugging a duffle bag around while I walked to Pop's.

Grumpy studied the cash on the counter, as if considering making an exception to the rule. "This is highly irregular. And quite possibly illegal. How do I know there is not a bomb in your bag?"

"There's no bomb."

"Did you say he has a bomb in his bag?" Sherlock Holmes asked.

"I don't have a bomb," I said.

Sherlock Holmes and Jessica Fletcher retreated to the far side of the parlor, which was all of like ten feet away.

"Please? It'll only be for a couple of hours," I said.

"We're not staying here if he has a bomb," Jessica Fletcher said.

"There's no bomb." I began unzipping my duffle bag.

She and Sherlock Holmes gasped loudly.

"Here, look for yourself." I dumped the contents of my duffle bag at my feet. "See? No bomb?"

Jessica Fletcher raised an eyebrow. "Could be in the liner."

"Or in his daypack," Sherlock Holmes added.

Grumpy sighed and then mumbled something about how much trouble it was when guests pay with cash. He opened the register drawer, made change, and handed me back ten dollars. I guess he figured my small daypack didn't warrant the full twenty-dollar fee. "I get off at seven. If you are not back by then, I cannot promise your things will still be here."

Before he could change his mind, I quickly stuffed my clothes and personal things back in my duffle.

More guests arrived. All were dressed as though they were on their way to a murder mystery dinner.

Maxwell Smart—the bumbling secret agent from the TV show *Get Smart*.

Frank Cannon—the overweight, balding ex-cop with a deep voice. He of the TV show *Cannon*.

Theo Kojak—the bald, lollipop-sucking, fedora-wearing police detective who was the lead character in (what else?) *Kojak*.

If you don't know who those characters are, ask your mom or dad or grandparents. They were popular TV detectives from the 1970s, when televisions were the size of a UPS truck and to change the channel you had to get up, walk across the room, and turn a knob.

Maxwell Smart, Frank Cannon, and Kojak formed a line behind me.

"I wouldn't get too close," said Jessica Fletcher. "He has a bomb."

Kojak rolled his lollipop to the other cheek. Maxwell Smart and Frank Cannon eyed me suspiciously.

The door opened. More guests arrived.

Cagney and Lacey, Charlie's Angels, and Columbo pushed their way into the parlor, which, in case you haven't figured out by now, was pretty crowded.

"OKAY, EVERYONE, QUIET DOWN!"

I zipped my duffle and looked up, but all I saw was Frank Cannon's broad backside.

"A few things to keep in mind before you head out and start investigating."

I straightened so I could see the person speaking. A deputy marshal stood in the doorway. He wore a white cowboy hat and heavy overcoat with a white fur collar. Sam McCloud from the TV series (you guessed it) *McCloud*.

"First, I don't want to hear any complaints any complaints from the witnesses or suspects. If they don't want to talk, respect their privacy."

Groans from the clot.

"I mean it. One complaint and I'll shut this down. Understood?"

Heads nodded.

"Second, if you visit the crime scene and it is roped off, stay behind the yellow tape."

More groaning.

"If I hear of one footprint inside the tape that's not supposed to be there, I'll shut down this investigation. Understood?"

Heads nodded but with less enthusiasm.

"Who made *him* sheriff?" Kojak grumbled.

"That would be Don Siegel," Frank Cannon replied.

"Most importantly, and I can't emphasize this enough, if you find or learn anything you think might be useful to the case, report it. Candee Brenneman's killer is still out there and we cannot get in the way of the official investigation. Understood?"

No heads nodded.

"UNDERSTOOD?"

Heads nodded reluctantly.

Jessica Fletcher pointed at me. "He has a bomb."

"I do not have a bomb."

"Who are you?" McCloud asked me.

"Isn't it obvious?" Cagney said. "He's Brandon Foster of *The Fosters.*"

"Who?" Lacey said.

"The oldest son. The biological one."

"He's definitely not Brandon Foster," said Columbo. "He's too young. And too short."

"Excuse me," I said, pushing past Frank Cannon. "I need to go visit someone."

"Look," Jessica Fletcher said loudly. "He's leaving his bag."

"And there's a bomb in it," Maxwell Smart said.

Then Columbo called out, "You need to claim your unattended—"

By that time, I was out the door. But it was clear that I would have some serious competition as I looked into the death of Candee Brenneman.

CHAPTER

3

A BEAST OF BIBLICAL PROPORTIONS

Bright Haven Retirement Community sat at the corner of Main and White streets. Across from the sprawling complex stood a five-story brick building that housed restaurants, shops, and apartments.

Urban living is the trend these days. Cities offer jobs, diversity, and a vibrant nightlife. Rural towns across America are dying. That's one reason Mom and Dad had decided to move to Savannah. Unless they wanted to work in Kansas City (a one-hour commute each way), both would have had to settle for working at a McDonald's or Starbucks or worse. In Dad's case, worse would have been some type of farm or ranch work. Most likely driving a truck delivering cattle.

I follow the curved driveway to Bright Haven's main entrance, passed through the automated doors, and stopped at the receptionist's desk.

"I'm here to see Herbert C. Hall."

On the guest register I signed in as *Nicholas Vedder*. Sometimes I'll sign my name Nick Faldo, Nick at Knight, or Nick of Time. It's a little joke I leave for the person coming after me.

"Can you find your way to his unit?" the receptionist asked.

"Last time I visited my grandfather, he was still living on Farrington Avenue."

"I'll get someone to walk you."

Minutes passed before a heavyset man with bushy sideburns and a nametag that read *Drake* entered the lobby. I followed Drake down a long wide hall decorated with paintings of ponds, sunsets, and waterfowl. The strong smell of pine-scented disinfectant made me wonder what type of odors they were trying to cover.

We exited onto a walkway that curved around a fountain, went through another set of doors, and entered the John J. Peterman wing. We stopped in front of 215.

Drake knocked and we waited.

And waited.

And …

Shuffling feet could be heard on the other side of the door. A dead bolt clanked, chain rattled. The door opened all of two inches.

Around the edge of the door, dusty blue eyes studied me. "Young man, if you came by to ask about your grade, you are wasting your time. I do not change grades. If you want a better grade, study harder."

I cast a sidelong glance at Drake.

He shrugged.

"I'm not here about my grade. You once told me that if I ever had questions about something that happened in the Bible, I should come see you."

I watched for a flicker of recognition, some hint that my grandfather knew me. It was hard to believe this was the same man who'd taught me how to tie a bowline, how to tie a bowtie, and how to park a boat. *Never come into the slip faster than you want to hit the dock.* His was the voice of Winnie the Pooh and the Cat in the Hat and Harry Potter.

And now my grandfather seemed to have no idea who I was.

"Sir, do you know this individual?" Drake asked.

My grandfather's gaze shifted from me to Drake and back. "Can you fix the Internet?"

"The Internet?" I asked.

"I called the number on that box, but I couldn't understand the person talking on the phone."

By box I assumed my grandfather meant his cable modem. "Mind if I take a look?"

Pop opened the door for me and stepped back. I mouthed *thanks* to Drake and went inside.

His small study looked exactly as I'd expected a religion professor's office to look. Books were stacked on bookcases, stacked on the floor, stacked in chairs. Hanging on the wall behind a badly worn wooden desk were framed black-and-white photos of the Jordan River, the Sea of Galilee, and the Wailing Wall. A window overlooked the fountain Drake and I had walked past.

My grandfather pointed at the black plastic box on the lower shelf of the bookcase. "When I moved in, they told me I needed the Internet to watch TV. Back on Farrington Avenue, all Marge and I used was an antenna. It worked. This blasted thing hardly ever works."

There was tape on the bridge of his Harry Truman glasses, and his thick shock of white hair had the disheveled look of someone who didn't own a comb.

"Does your TV still work?"

"Do you think I would own a television that didn't work?"

I took a knee and studied the row of status lights on his cable modem. "All five should be solid or flashing. You only have the two lit up."

He stood behind me, hands behind his back. "Can you fix it? When Marge gets back, she's going to want to watch *General Hospital.*"

My heart broke to think that this was the same man who'd let me sit in his lap while we drove down Main Street in his Oldsmobile Delta 88 convertible. And I didn't have the heart to mention to Pop that Grandma had died almost two years earlier. Her funeral was the last time I'd visited my grandfather. Which meant I'd probably already met Mom's friend Isobel, though I couldn't recall doing so.

I reached behind the cable modem and unplugged the power cord, counted to fifteen, and plugged it back in. Only one light came back on. I yanked the power cord out and waited longer this time.

Pop settled into his swivel office chair. "I warned my students years ago that the Internet would be the end of literacy and rational thinking. Now look where we are. A body can't even watch TV when it wants to."

"No worries, Pop. We'll get it fixed."

I powered up the modem a second time and silently hoped a full reboot would do the trick. While I waited, I took a seat in the chair across from him.

"I don't know if you remember, but one time you read me a story about someone in the Bible who got turned into a werewolf. Do you remember that?"

Pop eyed me suspiciously as if trying to make the connection. Off came the Truman glasses. He pulled a pair of readers from his shirt pocket. "King Nebuchadnezzar. Except it wasn't a wolf. Bible doesn't say what kind of animal it was."

"But he was turned into something, right?"

He reached over to the bookshelf beside his desk and pulled down a Bible. There was silver duct tape on the spine and sticky notes poking out between pages.

"I looked, and there before me was a holy one, a messenger, coming down from heaven. He called in a loud voice: 'Let the stump and its roots, bound with iron and bronze, remain in the ground, in the grass of the field. Let him be drenched with the dew of heaven, and let him live with the animals among the plants of the earth. Let his mind be changed from that of a man and let him be given the mind of an animal, till seven times pass by for him.'"

He eyed the modem. "Is the TV working yet?"

One light flashed. "Let's give it a few more minutes."

"I should have brought those VHS tapes when we moved, but Marge complained we wouldn't have space to store them."

"Don't worry. We'll get your TV working, Pop."

For the first time since I arrived, his eyes brightened. "I remember reading you this story when you were maybe five. When I explained that a week in Bible prophecy is the same as one year, you asked me if you could come and stay with me for a week sometime. I remember thinking then that you were going to give your mother fits when you got older."

I checked the cable modem again. Two lights flashed on the box, then three. "That was the summer you let me sit in your lap and drive that Oldsmobile of yours."

"At all of ten miles an hour. You had a death grip on the steering wheel. When your mother found out, she was horrified."

"And she'd never have known if Wendy hadn't told on us."

"How is your sister?"

"Bossy."

Four of the five lights went from blinking to solid. Finally, the bottom light turned bright yellow. I stood. "Let's go see if your TV works now."

"I told you, there is nothing wrong with my television set."

Without replying, I followed him into the small living room. He picked up a remote and pointed at the TV.

The set powered on and a guest on a talk show appeared. With blood vessels bulging on his forehead, the man shouted at the host of the show about how the president was ruining America. A woman wearing a dark-blue business suit interrupted and began wagging her finger at the man.

I took the remote from Pop and muted the volume. "*Gunsmoke?*"

"And *Marcus Welby*. Marge likes that one. I think it's because she likes Robert Young."

I located a classic TV show channel and added both to his favorites list. "Next time hit this button, and all the shows you like will come up."

"For Pete's sake, I know how to use the channel guide." He studied me more closely. "Why does your nametag say Nicholas Vedder? Has another family adopted you?"

"I wanted to see if the receptionist would notice."

"Did she?"

"Guess she's not a fan of Washington Irving."

"Probably reads at a fifth-grade level," he said. "If she reads at all." With the television muted, Pop shuffled back down the hall toward his study.

"In that passage you read it mentioned being bound with iron and bronze. What was that about?"

"Some scholars think iron and bronze fetters were used to keep Nebuchadnezzar shackled in his palace during his seven years of insanity." Pop eased around his desk and paused to glance out the window, where sprays of water shot from the fountain below. "The king was locked away so he would not be a threat to those around him. Or himself," he added with a hint of sadness.

I wondered if that's how he felt living in his tiny apartment. "Do you believe that king was really turned into an animal?" I asked.

Pop carefully lowered himself into his chair. I wasn't sure which was louder, the creaking chair or his groan. "Speculating on something that happened over three thousand years ago without any historical evidence to back it up is both foolish and reckless."

"But you must have an opinion. You know more about the Bible than anybody I know."

The readers went back on. Fingers turned pages.

Immediately what had been said about Nebuchadnezzar was fulfilled. His body was drenched with the dew of heaven until his hair grew like the feathers of an eagle and his nails like the claws of a bird.

Pausing, he looked across the desk at me. "Perhaps it was the part about the claws and hair that made you think he was turned into a wolf."

"But it happened, right? This isn't like one of those, whaddya call them, fables?"

He peered at me over the top of his readers. "Parables. And no. The Book of Daniel is prophetic literature. That means some of what you read happened, but other events will happen at some future time. Now if you are asking me if the king was changed into an animal, then I would say yes. According to the writings of Daniel, that would be considered an historical event. I have no reason to doubt the authenticity of this passage." Pop exchanged his readers for his taped-up Trumans and studied me more closely. "What is this really about? I know you did not come all this way simply to visit. Boys your age have better things to do with their time. Or should."

"A woman's body was found dead under a bridge a few weeks ago. There were large paw prints around her body. It happened during a full moon."

"And you think it might be a werewolf."

"I don't know what to think, Pop. It's just weird is all."

"People do not turn into animals and turn back again."

"But what you just read . . . I mean, if it happened once . . ."

"That was different. The king in that story offended God and was cursed."

"Offended God how?"

"He refused to acknowledge God as the ultimate authority on earth and heaven. Nebuchadnezzar claimed all his success was his own doing and that God had no part in it."

"So why couldn't it happen again? I mean, if a king or some other person offended God what's to stop him from turning that person into a wolf or lion?"

"It doesn't work that way."

"But why couldn't it work that way, that's what I'm asking."

He opened his desk drawer, riffled through a stack of business cards, and pushed one across the desk. "You should speak with someone who is knowledgeable in these matters."

I studied the name. "Sun Bear?"

"He knows the ways of the Wendigo. That is what his people call a man-wolf. If there is such a creature, Sun Bear will know."

"Let's say there was someone today going around acting the same way that king did. What sort of person would I be looking for?"

"Hypothetically speaking?"

"Yes."

"Rich. Powerful. Arrogant. Someone who doesn't respect people or God."

"Like the president, maybe?"

"It could be anyone, really, who has amassed influence and wealth and denies there is a God." He closed the drawer and, with a look of concern, said, "Mind if I give you some grandfatherly advice?"

"Fire away."

"Careful you do not go too far down this path. The Bible warns that those who practice witchcraft, speak to the dead, or perform sorcery are an affront to God. I'm not suggesting that's what you're doing, but this fascination with the supernatural could lead you into a dangerous place."

"I'll be careful, Pop, I promise."

"See that you are."

While he gazed at the framed pictures on the wall, I waited for him to say something else, to give me more grandfatherly advice.

Instead, he rose from his chair and removed a plaid, small-brim hat from the coat rack. "Now if you will excuse me, I need to be going. My class starts in a few minutes." He shouldered his small, wiry frame into a beige overcoat that seemed to swallow him. "I am sorry I cannot help you with your grade."

And just like that, my grandfather was gone, again.

"I'll study harder next time."

"See that you do."

On the curved driveway outside of Bright Haven, I braced myself against a biting wind. Clouds, thick and gray, had turned the late afternoon prematurely dark. There was a noticeable chill in the air and the smell of snow to come.

With hands in my pockets, I started walking back to the Headless Horseman.

I missed Pop. Missed his laughter and his simple but wise advice. I missed him making me feel important and loved and special. I wished I could do something to help him remember better, but maybe all I could do was visit more often. I promised myself I would.

When I entered the lobby of the Headless Horseman there was no sign of Grumpy or the '70s TV Sleuths. My clothes lay strewn on the floor in a corner behind a cushy high-back chair. I decided if Grumpy did return, I would definitely demand a refund on my baggage check.

From behind me the front door opened. A really hot-looking girl with a phone pressed to her ear walked in. She wore a white long-sleeved turtleneck sweater, black jeans, and gray calf-high suede boots.

"Found him, Mother. We'll meet you at Cellar 9." She ended the call and extended her hand to me. "Millie Canon, Izzy's daughter."

We shook. "Nick Caden."
"I know. And you're late. Let's go."

Chapter

4

MY NEW PARTNER IN CRIME

"**M**other is about to have a hissy fit. How come you didn't call to let her know you'd arrived?"

The hostess at Cellar 9 Bistro had seated us at a table beside a crackling wood fire. In a booth behind Millie sat a couple, their faces almost touching. A single long stem rose lay by the woman's plate. Three men sat at the bar, nursing beers. Muddy soles of brown boots rested on footrests. Leather coats with fur collars hung on the backs of bar chairs.

"I needed to see someone first," I said. "That's why I didn't call right away."

Millie removed her wool toboggan and fluffed her hair. "Your grandfather, I know." Scarf and blue overcoat went on the chair next to her. "You still could have called."

"I forgot," I said.

"That's no excuse."

I'd only known her for like, ten minutes, and already she had me wishing I'd snuck into the tire well of Dad's plane and flown back with him.

A waitress arrived and set menus in front of us. "Can I get you two something to drink?" She was a slight dark-skinned woman with cropped, curly hair. Her nametag read *Tickle*.

I study people, make mental notes. It's what you do when someone has tried to kill you. I want eyes in the back of my head but settle for constantly looking over my shoulder. I know that sounds like I'm exaggerating, but you try holding your breath for two minutes with a killer standing over top of you and see if you don't get a little paranoid.

"Diet soda," she said.

"Water with lemons."

The waitress trundled off to get our drinks.

"So how's your grandfather?" Millie asked.

"How did you know about that?"

"Desk clerk at the Headless Horseman. He said you asked directions for how to get to Bright Haven. You were supposed to come straight to our place." And just like that we were back to talking about how I was in trouble with Mom's childhood best friend.

I peered over the top of my menu. "We should probably order. What do you like on your pizza?"

She opened her menu. "I'm good with anything but anchovies."

"How about pepperoni?"

She frowned. "Anything but anchovies and pepperoni."

"Beef and cheese?"

"Are we ordering pizza or a hamburger?"

Tickle returned with my water and a diet soda. She plopped down a basket of breadsticks and removed a steno pad from her waistband. "Have you two decided?"

"Can I get some lemons for my water?" I said.

"Oh, sorry. Be right back."

I waited until Tickle was out of sight, then dunked my fork in my glass and swirled it around. When I looked up, Millie was staring at me. It was not a friendly stare. "There's a reason the nicer restaurants bring silverware in napkins," I said. "It keeps the utensils from touching the table. You wouldn't believe how many germs are on the average table rag."

"Oh … kay, but that doesn't explain why you're rinsing your fork in your glass."

"In a lot of places, the kitchen staff doesn't even bother to rinse dish trays before putting them in the dishwasher. All that soggy dough gets slung around and sticks on plates and glasses and forks."

"You're weird."

Like she was the first hot girl to ever tell me that.

I dried my fork on my napkin, then said, "Sign out front said today's special is Hawaiian."

"Pork on a pizza?"

"Tell you what, you pick."

"No, dinner is on me. Your choice."

Tickle returned and placed a saucer of lemons next to my glass. "Made a decision yet?"

"Double cheese with extra marinara sauce," I said. "Thin crust." I lifted my glass to show the bits of pizza dough floating around. "And can I get a new water?"

"Oh, goodness, of course."

Millie rested her elbows on the table and leaned forward, closing the gap between us. "How did you do it, exactly?"

"Do what?"

"Solve those murders." I guess she saw the surprised look on my face because she added, "Mother told me that's your hobby."

"I wouldn't call it a hobby, exactly."

"But you identified a couple of killers, right? And they got arrested and charged? Mother wasn't making that up?"

"First, after I've gathered all the facts about the case I can find, I build a profile with the data. Time, location, condition of the body, names of anyone mentioned in news stories that might have some connection to the victim. Then I run a versatile statistical analysis algorithm for the detection of aberrations."

"You do what to who?"

My new water glass arrived. I squeezed in two lemons and stirred with my knife. "Check for trends that might point to who committed the murder and why. A lot of shows hire crime consultants. That means what you see on a TV may have actually happened. It also means that some people will act out on what they see. That's how I figured out who shot the actor playing Jessie James in Deadwood Canyon. At the time it didn't even occur to me that I'd seen a similar episode during the first season of *Badlands*. I only had a hunch and I acted on it."

"For real? You can do that?"

"But it's not just me. I'm part of a group called TV Detectives."

"Hey, I've seen them around town!"

"Different group," I said. "We have a huge database of shows. When we started there were only a few of us. Now we have members all over the world. We binge on shows, catalog each episode scene by scene, and load it all into the database. Of course, getting law enforcement to take us seriously is a whole different deal."

"I would think so." She tossed her bangs back, which I took to be a good sign. I had read some place that a girl tossing back her hair may be an invitation and a sign she may be warming up to you.

Pathetic, I know, but when you're a tall, gangly kid with pimples and sprigs of hair on your chin and absolutely no chance of penetrating the popular and pretty girls clot in your school you need all the positive signs you can get.

"Did you read the newspaper clipping Mother sent?"

"A werewolf didn't kill that woman. There's no such thing."

"Don't be so sure." She pulled her phone from her purse and swiped its screen. "Read this."

When I took the phone, her thumb brushed the side of my hand and I felt my cheeks turn red. I'm sure she noticed.

October 30, Sleepy Hollow, New York: Sometime last week, having traveled the Appalachian Trail from its starting point at Springer Mountain in Georgia, Robert Kincaid exited the trail near Bear Mountain, New Jersey. From there he hitched a ride to Peekskill,

New York, and caught a southbound commuter train to Sleepy Hollow. Witnesses later recalled seeing Kincaid near a bridge in Rockefeller State Park taking pictures of the Pocono River. Though camping in the park is illegal, this week a fourth grader on a school field trip found what is believed to be Kincaid's blood-soaked sleeping bag at Raven Rock not far from the bridge. As with the attack on Candee Brenneman last month, large paw prints were found in the area. Authorities continue to list Kincaid as a missing person.

"Look at the date," Millie said. "It happened exactly one month after the first attack. Both occurred during full moons. And there were large wolf prints found both times."

"It's not a werewolf. Dog maybe, but not a monster."

"You watch," Millie said, "this backpacker's body will show up someplace and when they find it it'll be ripped apart."

I don't know why people want to believe the worst will happen but they do.

From behind Millie's chair a woman in pearls and heels approached us. "Oh my word, would you look at this? Why, you're the spitting image of your father."

"Nick, this is my mother," Millie said. "Mother, Nick."

Mrs. Canon wore long white gloves that reached all the way up to her elbows, a white frou-frou velvet hat with a cluster of feathers tucked in one side, and a crimson dress that fitted her so tightly that all three men at the bar stared. And kept staring. As did some of the men who were there with their dates.

"You think I look like Dad?" I said.

"No question. You have his dimpled chin and regal nose."

Right then I wondered if maybe Mom was right to be a little concerned about Dad and her childhood best friend.

"Have you two ordered?"

"Just now. Nick couldn't make up his mind what kind of pizza he wanted." Millie smiled at me.

Hers was a good smile. Straight white teeth. I bet she uses a professional for bleaching.

"I'll ask them to make the order to go," Mrs. Canon said. "The roads are beginning to get icy."

While I hooked my daypack strap over my shoulder, Millie asked me if I had ever heard of Silas Long.

"Who?"

"Silas Long is buried in the Sleepy Hollow Cemetery. If there's time, you should check out his grave."

For a couple of seconds, she stood beside her chair, eyeing her coat, like she expected it to float up and onto her shoulders. Then like a klutz I realized she was waiting for me to help her put it on.

Which I did.

When she flipped her hair off her collar I smelled raspberry-scented shampoo. So in addition to being rich and pretty and sort of bossy she also smelled nice.

"The headstone says, 'Here lies Silas Long, half man and half wolf.'"

"That's important why?" I asked.

"And you call yourself a TV detective. I can see you're going to need someone to help you find the Sleepy Hollow werewolf."

I did not need someone to help me find the Sleepy Hollow werewolf. But of course I didn't say that because by that point I was under the spell of raspberry-scented shampoo.

Like an idiot I said, "Good idea."

Then from across the room someone yelled, "THAT'S HIM. THAT'S THE BOY WITH THE BOMB IN HIS BAG!"

If you guessed that someone was Jessica Fletcher you would be right.

The cast of the '70s TV Sleuths quickly filed into the bistro, so before Millie and everyone else in the restaurant could see that Jessica Fletcher was pointing at me, I bolted for the back door.

Chapter

5

THE CANON CASTLE

If you are thinking, as I was, that Millie Canon and her mom lived in a large home overlooking a golf course with maybe a view of the country club, you'll be disappointed to know that I underestimated how rich they were.

The Canons lived in a castle. No kidding, a real honest-to-goodness replica of the Blair Castle in Scotland. Thirty rooms in all. Each furnished with period pieces and furniture. Family portraits and landscape paintings hung on walls; Scottish military uniforms and weapons adorned mannequins. In the ballroom alone there were seventy-five pairs of antlers. Elk, caribou, deer, gazelle ... you get the point.

The Canons housed their guests in bedrooms located in the Tower Turret: a circular silo-type structure that anchored one corner of the enormous home.

"This place reminds me of the Biltmore," I said.

"You've been to the Biltmore?"

"Last summer. Someone found a dead vampire on a golf course in Transylvania, North Carolina. After I solved the murder, we spent a few days in Asheville."

"Vampire?"

"I'll explain later."

Millie hung her scarf, coat, and toboggan in a front door closet that was half the size of my bedroom back in Kansas. She then joined me at the foot of a staircase the width of an interstate highway. Her clothes smelled of melting snow and wood fire. For reasons I can't explain, I found myself imagining how much fun the two of us would have camping in the woods.

"If you like large, ornate, and luxurious homes you can't actually, you know, enjoy," she said, "you'll love it here."

"You kidding me? I think this place is awesome."

"How many castles have you spent the night in?"

"Me? None."

"And neither have any of my friends. At least not since … " She turned her face away and thumbed her eyes.

I could tell she was about to cry, so I did what I always do in situations where I have no idea what to say to a girl who is obviously having an emotional moment—I said something stupid. "So … those animals mounted on the wall, did your dad kill them all?"

She whirled, trotted to the hall bathroom, and locked the door behind her, leaving me standing at the bottom of the staircase, feeling like an even bigger idiot than before. When she emerged after, like, five minutes, she had magically transformed herself back into a put-together pretty, rich girl. Other than one small spot of runny mascara around her left earlobe, I would have never guessed she'd been crying.

Of course I still had no idea why.

"No sleepovers, no birthday parties," she said. "Oh, at first my friends are all excited about visiting."

We were back to talking about me staying at the Canons'.

"Who wouldn't be? This place looks like what I'd always picture Gryffindor might look like in the Harry Potter books."

"But when my friends' parents find out they have to sign a waiver saying they and their child are responsible for anything they damage during the stay, they change their mind. You're the first person to stay in our home since, like, forever."

"But your mom didn't make me sign anything."

"That's because Mother knows your mom. There's something there, not sure what, but I think Mother owes your mom big time for something that happened years ago."

"Still, I mean, you live in a castle."

"Believe me, living in a museum with just your mother isn't all that it is cracked up to be. Come on, I'll show you where you're staying."

We entered one of the bedrooms off the hallway.

I should explain here that the word *bedroom* in a castle means something different than *bedroom* in a normal house. In a normal house you might have a closet in your bedroom, and if you're really lucky, your own bathroom.

Inside the two double doors, we strolled passed a sitting parlor that also served as a study, then crossed the gigantic bedroom and went through a changing area with shelves and closets for clothes.

Finally, we reached a bathroom the size of a Starbucks.

Millie pointed at a narrow door cut into the paneled wall beside some empty shelves. "Your room is that way."

"You mean I'm not sleeping here?"

Laughing, she said, "You must be kidding. Mother has a cot set up for you in the attic."

We entered the door and climbed a twisting staircase.

She walked ahead of me, her flashlight's beam aimed upward at the rickety stairs. "Mother said someone tried to kill you?"

"I wish she hadn't said that. It's not something we want a lot of people to know."

"But you are dead, right? At least, officially."

"Sort of. I have a grave and headstone in Kansas. Obviously I've never seen it. My sister and parents drove back after it happened and held a funeral for me. My friends and some family came. Mom and dad felt bad about lying to them. Still do. But until the guy who tried to kill me is caught it's better if everyone thinks I'm dead."

"But I know you're not. And Mother knows."

"Which is why I'm surprised she said anything. Mom must have trusted your mother to keep quiet."

"Are you in witness protection?"

"My parents and I talked about it, but Witsec is a huge inconvenience. So instead I'm extra careful. Like back at the bistro, you may have noticed that I wiped down my fork and knife before we left."

"You did that before you ate too."

"Yeah, but for different reasons. Even something as small as a water glass can have my prints on it, and I can't risk that."

"Because the man who tried to kill you could still be out there looking?"

"Exactly."

Once we reached the top of the wobbly wooden landing, Millie pressed down on a thumb latch and pushed open a mouse-hole-shaped door. Cobwebs clung to dusty rafter beams above my so-called cot.

When you hear the word *cot*, you may envision— oh, I don't know—a collapsible camp bed with maybe a pillow. Here the word *cot* means thin mattress on dirty hardwood floors in a cramped attic with only a tiny window looking out.

"I'm sleeping … in here?"

"Trust me, it's worse than it looks. There are bats. And rats. Oh, and it's not heated." Millie remained on the landing as though reluctant to venture inside. "You may wish to hang your suitcase and daypack on those nails in the rafters."

"You can't be serious."

"Oh, I'm dead serious. Mother has rules. And rule number one is no one *sleeps* on the furniture. No one *puts* anything on the furniture. No one *touches* the furniture. You're the only person I know who would agree to sleep in a haunted attic with rats and bats."

"Wait, did you say haunted?"

"Don't worry. I've never seen the ghost. Mother says she has. But then Mother also hears voices." Millie started to leave, then turned back. "I have my tutoring classes in the morning, but I'm usually done by lunch. If you want, we can go to Rockefeller State Park and see if we can find the bridge where that woman died."

"Assuming rats, bats, and ghosts don't get me first."

She smiled.

Did I mention she had what I'm sure were professionally bleached-white teeth?

"Don't worry. I was mostly kidding about the ghosts. Night, Nick."

She pulled the door shut behind her.

Other than the light of a full moon outside the small attic window, my room was totally dark. If I could relive that moment again, I would run. Bolt from the attic, scamper down the stairs, and race back to Pop's, begging him to let me sleep on his couch.

But I didn't.

Instead, I crept to the window and peered through ice-encrusted panes.

It was then that I heard what I'm almost sure was a wolf's howl.

Chapter

6

MY COVER IS BLOWN

By some miracle I slept through the night without getting my toes nibbled off by rats or neck bitten by bats.

Breakfast at the Canon Castle was fresh fruit, yogurt, and tofu.

Tofu, in case you do not know, is bean curd. To me *tofu* sounds like something my sister Wendy might wear to a dance recital. I picked a peach from a bowl, and Mrs. Canon cut it into small pieces for me.

"Add some tofu," she said. "I made it myself."

"I'll pass."

"You should really have a bowl. It helps keep your system clean."

Here I should point out that having a conversation with my mom's childhood best friend about my *system* wasn't something I felt comfortable discussing.

"He said he doesn't want any, Mother."

I shot Millie an appreciative look. At least I hope she took it that way.

"But you're having some," she said to Millie. "After all, your doctor said girls at your age going through their—"

"MOTHER!"

I offered my saucer. "Peach?"

Millie hurried out of the kitchen and locked herself in the hall bathroom.

"Your mother told me how you helped capture a cold-blooded killer in Wyoming." Izzy smiled. "Is that true?"

"It wasn't in Wyoming. And I didn't capture him. The sheriff did."

"But *you* found the killer. Is that correct?"

"I was the only one who knew there'd been a murder, so no one else was really looking. I guess you could say I got lucky."

Millie returned from the kitchen. A smudge of mascara remained on her temple and her eyes were red. She cut slices of a peach and dumped them in a cup of yogurt.

Mrs. Canon pushed the dish of tofu at me. "If you sprinkle cheese on it, it tastes like pizza."

"Trust me," Millie said, "it tastes nothing like pizza."

"Forgive me for saying this," Mrs. Canon said, "but I find it hard to believe that someone your age without any law enforcement training could track down a cold-blooded killer on your own."

Millie stopped stirring her yogurt and turned to her mother. "Nick runs versatile statistical analysis to de-

tect similarities in certain types of murders. Researchers are using this technique to detect genomic aberrations in human cancer cells." Millie said to me, "After I
went to bed, I did a little reading on the web.

Mrs. Canon dabbed the corner of her mouth with
a napkin. "Why, that's the silliest thing I've ever heard
… watching TV to solve a murder. Does your mother
encourage this sort of behavior?"

"She likes that I have a hobby that provides a little income. I write for a paranormal news site. Or did.
The *Cool Ghoul Gazette*. I've identified the killer in five
cases so far. Three in which I was directly involved and
two by simply reviewing the case files. But like I told
your daughter, the hard part is getting anyone to believe me."

"I can imagine," Mrs. Canon said. "Was the man in
Wyoming the one who tried to drown you?"

"Deadwood isn't in Wyoming, but yes, he's the
one."

"It must have been difficult holding your breath
for such a long period of time. Your mother told me it
was close to five minutes."

"Mom exaggerates."

"But that man who tried to kill you is still after
you?"

"We're not sure. They still haven't found him, so I
suppose it's possible Patrick Gabrovski is still out there
looking for me." To Millie I said, "Remember how I
told you last night at the bistro that people will sometimes commit a crime they see on TV?"

"You called them copycat killings."

"Last spring a fourteen-year-old boy was in a
cross-country race in Alaska when he was mauled to

death by a black bear. At least that's how the incident was reported. The story was all over the news for a few days. Bear, gator, and shark attacks usually are. Weeks later, authorities announced that the boy had actually died from blunt-force trauma to the head. Black bears aren't normally meat eaters, but they will feed on a carcass. The autopsy report concluded that the bear mauled the boy hours after he died. They're still looking for his killer."

"Last night I told Nick about the grave of Silas Long," Millie said. "He's never heard the name."

"Well, dear, he is only in the—what grade are you in?"

"Ninth."

"Millie started the tenth this fall. She's a year ahead. We've already got her signed up online for a several college courses."

As if that made Millie smarter than me—which of course she was.

"The weird part is," I said, trying to move the conversation away from academics, "almost the exact same thing happened several seasons earlier in an episode of *Dread of Night*."

"It did?" Millie said.

I nodded. "Except in that episode the attack took place in the hills east of Hollywood in Runyon Canyon Park. Later in the show you find out it was a rival actor who is the killer. To make it look like an animal attack, he spread blood around the body to attract mountain lions. My guess is, whoever killed that boy had watched that episode of *Dread of Night*."

Mrs. Canon said, "I seriously doubt that there is a bear or mountain lion or wolf going around attacking people in Sleepy Hollow."

"I'm with you there, Mrs. Canon."

"Call me Izzy."

I nodded politely, even though I had no intention of calling Mom's childhood best friend by her first name.

I finished off the peaches and pushed my chair back. "By chance can you give me a lift?" I asked Izzy. "There's someone I need to see."

"Mother, you can drop him off, right? After running me by my tutor's?"

"I wish I could, dear, but I have a meeting this morning. He can ride your bike. Unless he's uncomfortable riding a girl's bike."

Someone knocked on the front door.

Mrs. Canon went to the window and pulled back the curtain. "A Westchester County Police car is parked in the circle."

Another knock on the door, louder this time.

"Wonder what they want?"

I didn't say anything, but I had a sick feeling in my stomach.

Mrs. Canon went to the door and opened it. "Yes?"

"Are you Mrs. Canon?"

By that point Millie and I were peering around the corner into the hallway. I couldn't see the officer's face, but I could definitely see his hand on his holster.

"Yes. What's this about?"

"I'm investigating a complaint about a boy with a bomb. Is he here?"

Chapter

7

LEGEND OF THE WENDIGO

"What boy?"

"I don't know his name, ma'am. I have reason to believe that a boy with a bomb in his duffle bag left a restaurant with you last evening. Mind if I come in and check?"

"You have a bomb?" Millie whispered to me.

"No."

"So why does he think you do?"

"Long story."

"Do you have a warrant?" Mrs. Canon asked.

"I can go get a warrant if you want," the officer replied.

"I do not *want*. But if you insist, you will need one."

I had to hand it to Millie's mom—she wasn't one to get rolled easily.

"Or you could simply take my word that I am not housing a terrorist with a bomb."

"I never said he was a terrorist, ma'am."

"Do you know of many people who carry bombs in their duffle bag that are not?"

"Ah ... no, ma'am."

"Then believe me when I say there is no boy with a bomb in my house."

When she said *boy with a bomb in my house*, she almost shouted it, like: "THERE HAD BETTER NOT BE A BOY WITH A BOMB IN MY HOUSE, OR IF THERE IS, HE BETTER BE GONE THIS INSTANT."

Things were quiet for several seconds, then the officer spoke. "If you say the boy with the bomb isn't here, I'll take your word for it. Sorry for the inconvenience."

I could imagine him tipping his hat, walking back to his car, and probably wishing he'd never gotten the call to come to Canon Castle.

The front door slammed shut.

Mrs. Canon's heels clicked loudly on hardwood floors.

For like, two seconds, I thought about hanging around and answering Mrs. Canon's questions about the bomb that wasn't in my bag. But instead I hurried down to the carriage house with Millie.

Minutes later, I sped off on a pink girl's bike with a white wicker basket mounted over the front tire.

Sleet and freezing rain fell from a luminous gray sky. I checked the map app on my smartphone and followed the blue line until I reached 1 West Sunnyside Lane. A chain hung between two posts stretched across a gravel drive covered by icy slush. Hooked to the chain and dangling by one corner was a NO TRESPASSING sign. I ditched the bike behind a large cedar.

After walking under a tunnel of sagging evergreen branches crusted over with ice, I emerged from the woods. Across the white meadow stood a stone cottage, its chimney belching smoke.

A burly man sprouting a thick beard came around the corner, pushing a wheelbarrow loaded with firewood. His black ponytail snaked down the back of a plaid flannel shirt. Jean pants rode over work boots.

"Sun Bear?"

With the back of his hand, he bumped up the brim of his beige cowboy hat. Small brown eyes studied me from beneath bushy brows. I hoped he was not armed. He looked like the type who might be.

"My grandfather said I should stop by."

His gaze shifted from me to the gravel drive and back. He scooped up an armload of wood, climbed the steps, and bumped open the front door with the toe of his boot. "If you're waiting for an invite, you just missed it," he said, leaving the door open behind him.

Inside the cottage, which smelled of fresh-cut wood and leather furniture, a large room with a vaulted ceiling took up most of the downstairs. A spiral staircase in a back corner led to a loft over the kitchen. I wouldn't have thought the small stone cottage large enough for two levels, but by dropping the ceiling, it worked.

"Tea?" he asked, hanging his hat on a nail tacked to a wooden beam.

"Yes, please."

He set two mismatched mugs on the kitchen counter and dropped a tea ball in one. "Prof warned me I should keep an eye out for a lanky kid who might look lost."

His comment surprised me. I hadn't been exactly sure Pop would even remember me coming by. "He has trouble remembering things."

"With Prof, there's more to forget. Smartest man I ever met."

I made my way over to the hearth and stood with my back to the fireplace, palms exposed to the flames. "I'm trying to figure out your accent. Doesn't sound like the New Yorkers I've heard."

He poured hot water into a mug. "Texas by way of North Dakota. I was born a few miles south of the Canadian border in a place called Bowbells. Population three hundred fifty-nine. Honey?"

"Yes, please."

"My mother's people are Chippewa. My old man worked rigs in the States. That's how come I get to be a US citizen. My old man kept chasing work till he died. Rigging is a tough way to make a living." He handed me my tea.

I cradled the mug, warming my hands.

"I still speak the language. Not like I used to, but if you give me enough peyote, I can gin up a pretty good rain dance. How's the tea?"

I sipped. "Hot." I took a bigger slurp, enjoying the shock of heat as it warmed my throat. "How did you end up here?"

"Oil. Followed in the old man's footsteps. Barrel price kept dropping and rigs kept shutting down. That's when I came east. Answered an ad for a maintenance mechanic job at the local college." He eased into a recliner with stuffing poking through the armrest. "Prof said you had questions about the Wendigo?"

"Is there really such a creature?"

He shrugged. "My ancestors knew its ways. Had an uncle on Mom's side who told stories bout how he'd avoid the Black Forest during full moons. Said it wasn't safe to be out at night. He did some trapping up in Alberta. Used to brag about how he once got mauled by a brown bear. He knew a thing or two about surviving in the wild. Went for months sometimes living on nothing other than what he trapped and killed. Saw bears, wolves, mountain lions … maybe even Sasquatch for all I know. Never saw the Wendigo. Don't mean it's not out there, though."

"How do you know my grandfather?"

"Local college. After I took the maintenance job, they put me in charge of landscaping. Prof used to come outside to sit and read. I thought I'd finally found steady work when I got that job at the college. In the oil business, you put in long hours, save all you can, and ride out the lean years. But there were budget cuts at the college. That's when I took this job as the grounds keeper at Sunnyside."

"Sunnyside?"

"Don't you know where you are, boy? This is part of the estate of that famous author." He pointed out the window. "I can't take you over to the man's home. They charge for that. But I can show you round the property that's not on the tour."

I followed him out the front door and to the back of the cabin. Parked underneath the extended roof of a work shed was a late '50s or early '60s rust-colored pickup—a relic from a time when trucks rolled off American assembly lines with chrome bumpers, curved fenders, and running boards. I'd seen a picture of Pop and his father beside one.

Next to the truck sat lawn equipment. Zero-radius riding lawn mower, rototiller, wood splitter. Rakes, hoes, and shovels hung on the wall beside an edger and weed eater.

Sun Bear pointed past the shed toward the trees. "When I moved in, there was an old storage shed back in those woods. One whole side of it was shot to pieces like somebody used it for target practice. There's supposed to be a stone bench in there where the author went to sit and think. Never found it. Makes for a good story, though."

I stomped my feet to try and get the blood flowing. "If there *were* such a creature as this Wendigo, what would it look like?"

"It's big as a man. Hunts at night mostly. Meat eater. Feeds on deer, bison, elk … anything large and fast."

"So a person jogging …"

"Would be seen as prey. You're talking about something that's got the mind of a man and the instincts of a wolf. Fast and powerful. By the time you saw it, it would be too late."

We had arrived at a greenhouse. Inside were two rows of poinsettias, their leaves bright red. Nearby a large pile of black potting soil reached almost to the roof.

Sun Bear must have noticed me staring at the poinsettias because he said, "They're for Christmas tours of the estate. I'm supposed to deliver them over to the home this week."

"Okay," I said. I admit this wasn't a great response, but I didn't know what else to say. "The Wendigo, how would it react to someone camping in the woods?"

"Like any wolf, it's territorial. It would see a camper as a threat. You cold?"

"I'm fine."

"That's what people say when they're lying."

We slowly made our way back to the front porch.

"How would someone go about becoming a Wendigo?" I said.

"You'd need a shaman to cast the spell. That's how it happened the first time. A medicine man living up in Wisconsin near the Canadian border came across a young teen who had killed a deer. After the two shared a meal, the shaman rewarded the boy for his kindness by giving him the ability to change into a wolf."

"And if someone were bitten?"

"By it and lived? They wouldn't be turned into a Wendigo, if that's what you're thinking. There'd have to be some kind of evil inside 'em. Take that boy. He was already an expert hunter. Could track and kill just fine, but he wanted to be more. He wanted power."

"Changed him how?"

"Got to where he fought all the time. Couldn't keep from taunting his rivals. Then one time a bigger boy got the best of him in a fight. Instead of fighting fair, the boy turned into a wolf. Ripped his rival's throat apart. Yanked arms from sockets. Disemboweled the victim. After that, the shaman put a curse on the boy so he could only access the wolf spirit during full moons."

We worked our way back to the shed and stopped beside the old pickup. You rarely see trucks like this on the road anymore. Pop told me one time that when he was my age, he could tell the make and model of a truck coming down the road by the sound of its engine. He also told me Detroit's downward slide began during the first gas crisis back in the '70s. "People waited in line for hours to fill up, and you could only get gas on certain days of the week. After that, foreign cars and trucks flooded the market."

Sun Bear opened the driver's door. "Hop in."

Stepping onto the running board I eased myself onto a sun-cracked leather seat. I rested my wrist on the steering wheel and studied the ice-glazed windshield. The frozen coating made interesting shapes on the glass. "How would someone go about finding such a creature?"

"Same as you would any large animal. Only difference is, you're hunting something that's got animal instincts and the mind of a man. It's as smart as you are. Smarter, actually. Tracking it would be nearly impossible."

"And if I did find one? What then?"

"Shoot it. Don't hesitate. Kill it before it kills you."

I reached for the round wooden shift knob. "Any way to trap it?"

"Wouldn't recommend you try. You're talking about something that's pure evil. A thing without a soul."

"Oh, there you are!"

Surprised, I leaned around the door jamb and looked across the field. Millie Canon came marching toward us from the woods, pushing the bike I'd left hidden. She had on a wool toboggan with a gray scarf tucked into the collar of her blue overcoat. L.L.Bean Duck Boots left small footprints in the snow.

Sun Bear said, "Friend of yours?"

"Not sure."

Millie brushed past Sun Bear and leaned into the truck. "They found him."

"Found who?"

"Robert Kincaid. Or what's left of him. We need to go see the medical examiner, like now." Millie took my elbow, pulling me from the truck.

"Kill it?" I said to Sun Bear.

"Before it kills you."

Chapter

8

BODY OF EVIDENCE

Sun Bear drove with earbuds in, his phone tucked in the breast pocket of his flannel shirt. Each time he stomped the accelerator pedal, the truck let out a deep-throated roar, which made me smile a little.

I sat in the passenger seat, Millie in the middle scrunched up close next to me.

"Nice of him to give us a lift," I said.

"As if taking ride-share would have been too hard," she said.

"With your pretty pink bike sticking out of the trunk like we're leaving a yard sale?"

"We'd have managed."

I had the impression Millie wasn't a fan of old trucks. Or maybe she wasn't a fan of old trucks with really small front seats where the person sitting next to her was basically in her lap.

"What were you two talking about back there?" she asked.

"Nothing."

"Didn't sound like nothing."

"Aren't you supposed to be at your tutor's?"

"My session got cancelled. His daughter's school has a two-hour delay due to icy roads. Come on, tell me … who are you going to shoot?"

"No one."

"Are you going to blow them up with a bomb?"

"How come you don't go to private school?" I asked, changing the subject.

"I did for a while. But then Mother said for the same amount of money I could learn just as much and more with private tutors. Me and four others study together. I take all my exams at an accredited testing facility in Manhattan."

"You ever tried public?"

"Once. For a week. I got picked on something terrible."

Sun Bear swung the pickup into a parking space on a side street. The Westchester County Medical Examiner's Office was a beige single-story building with no windows. While Millie approached the nondescript metal door marked ENTRANCE, I grabbed her bike from the truck's bed.

Sun Bear rehooked the chains on the truck's tailgate and turned toward me. "Watch yourself. The Wendigo is nothing to make light of."

"I'll be careful."

"I'd hate to think our little chat caused you to do something stupid."

As if I needed help in that department. I rolled Millie's bike to the cement stoop and waited while Millie pressed an intercom button.

"What makes you think the ME is going to see us?" I said.

"She knows Mother. Mother was a big contributor to the mayor's last campaign. The ME owes her job to the mayor."

Millie punched the button again. "So … who are you going to shoot and blow up?"

The girl was tenacious—a word Mom often used to describe my sister. "The Wendigo."

She turned all the way around to face me. "What's that?"

Thankfully the door opened partway. "Yes?"

"My mother, Isabel Canon, talked with someone about the body that was found this morning?"

A woman in light blue scrubs opened the door all the way. "I haven't done a full examination yet. This is part-time." She flipped through pages in her metal clipboard. "I should get to the autopsy this afternoon."

"But you think it's Robert Kincaid?" I said.

"I wouldn't want to speculate."

"How about the other victim," I asked. "The person they found under that bridge two months ago?"

The ME flipped to the back of her clipboard. "Candice Brenneman. Caucasian female. Age thirty-three. No children. The victim suffered a fracture of the posterior elements of C3 and C4."

"C3 and C4?" Millie said.

"Her neck was broken, but that's not what killed her."

"No?"

"She died from blood loss. There was a deep, ragged tear along the right side of her throat that severed her carotid artery."

I said to Millie, "The newspaper clipping your mom sent didn't mention that."

"The police asked us to keep it quiet," said the ME. "Her clothes showed vertical distribution of blood."

"How about the bite marks? Anything interesting there?"

"There were elevated levels of the enzymes lysozyme and peroxidase in the tissue around the wound."

"So possibly a dog attack," Millie said. "Or wolf."

"I don't know about a wolf but a large dog is definitely a possibility."

"Anything else that might be helpful?" I asked.

"The victim still wore a sapphire ring on her right hand, gold chain necklace, and diamond stud earrings. No signs of sexual assault." The ME closed her clipboard. "I should be getting back."

Millie said, "Who identified the body?"

She skimmed a page. "Butch Prescott. Her boss at GetFit Gym."

The door closed.

Millie said to me, "Where to next?"

"The bridge where Brenneman was found."

"I'd love to come with you, but I need to get to my tutor. Can you wait until I'm finished?"

"How long will that take?"

"Not that." Her eyes suddenly went wide. "Oh hey! Here's an idea. Why don't you ride to the Westchester County Municipal Golf Course and find Uncle Joe."

"Uncle Joe?"

"My father's brother."

"You sure the course is open today? With the snow and all?"

"Oh goodness, yes. People around here would play golf in a blizzard if they'd let them. Find Uncle Joe and have him drive you to the bridge where that woman was found. I'll meet you there at, say, noonish?"

"Sure ... I guess. But how will I find your uncle?"

"Trust me, that won't be a problem."

Chapter

9

UNCLE JOE

At the edge of the ninth fairway of the Westchester County Municipal Golf Course, a man in a silk maroon bomber jacket with the words *BAGGER JOE* printed across the back was parked in a collapsible aluminum chair with his head back, mouth open, eyes closed.

Spittle glistened in his wiry beard. Rolled-up gray sweatpants barely covered his knees. A dingy pair of double-striped tube socks poked out of brown work boots. He could have easily passed as a trespassing vagrant. From over the crest of a rise in the fairway came the *ping* of a golf club head striking a ball.

A white dot arched against a slate-colored sky with the high loft of a seven or eight iron. The ball easily cleared the small creek, hit the cart path, and rolled to a stopped in front of his chair. With eyes closed, he nudged it with the toe of his boot.

"Uncle Joe?" I said.

His eyes remained closed. "Who's asking?"

"I'm a friend of Millie's."

"Cyrus or niece. I'm acquainted with both."

"Millie Canon."

A gas-powered golf cart bumped across the wooden bridge and sputtered to a stop. The driver wore an orange ball cap, orange pullover sweater, and crisp gray golf slacks—an obvious nod to golfing pro Rickie Fowler.

Uncle Joe approached the man. "You hooked it," he said. "Had plenty of distance, but you probably came out of your swing too early. Next time make sure to keep your head down and don't release your grip until you've reached the ten o'clock position. Oh, and play the pin more to the right." He reached for Rickie Fowler's club. "May I?"

Rickie Fowler recoiled. "NO!"

Uncle Joe shrugged. "Your loss. First lesson is free. Here's the first lesson. Never trust your instincts when a club pro gives you free advice."

Uncle Joe handed Rickie Fowler a *Uncle Joe* flyer printed on hot pink paper.

Rickie Fowler balled it up and threw it in the creek.

"Change your mind, call me." Uncle Joe wandered back over and dropped into his chair.

Rickie Fowler waggled his iron, shifting his weight from left to right.

"From here, you'll want to lay up," Uncle Joe said as Rickie Fowler continued waggling his club back and forth. "Because with that club in this wind"— Rickie Fowler drew back—"you might hit it fat."

Rickie Fowler swung, carving a deep divot in the turf, splattering mud onto his golf shoes. The ball soared over the green, a retention pond, a Porta-John, and a chain-link fence before disappearing into traffic on the road next to the course.

"And send it out of bounds."

Rickie Fowler pounded the head of his club into the grass and muttered some bad words, jumped into his golf cart, and sped off.

"HAVE A NICE DAY!" Uncle Joe called after him.

On the highway beside the golf course, tires bled rubber, bumpers bounced off guardrails. Radiators hissed. Glass tinkled. Horns blared.

Uncle Joe glanced back at me. "You know my niece?"

"We met yesterday. I'm staying at the Canons'."

From our right came the sweet *ping* again of a metal head striking a ball. The white dot split the sky and landed with a thud next to the snow-covered creek.

"Millie told me you could give me a ride to RIP's," I said.

"Sure, why not?" Uncle Joe jabbed a thumb back toward a dense cluster of trees. "My rig is parked over there beside that maintenance shed."

Now, in my mind the word *rig* means a vehicle of some kind with wheels and possibly a motor. Maybe even a truck. Uncle Joe's *rig* was a horse-drawn buggy.

"You Amish?"

"Was."

Another golf cart raced toward us. A large man wearing a short-sleeved lime-green golf shirt rocked the cart as he exited. His large apple-round belly sagged over paisley print golf pants. The tips of his blond hair, darkened with sweat, brushed buffalo-wide shoulders. He stood with fists on hips, eyes scanning the fairway.

"Next time use a five iron," Uncle Joe said. "Relax that gorilla grip and let the club do the work."

Paisley Print slapped ice-encrusted weeds with his club. "Do you know who I am?"

"I know who you used to be, but those days of winning majors at Crooked Stick and the Old Course are long gone. Now it's just you, the course, and the ball. And yours is lost." Uncle Joe handed him a flyer.

Paisley Print crushed it in his huge mitt and threw it at Uncle Joe's chest.

"I also offer anger management therapy." Uncle Joe returned to his chair. "Golf instruction is a cut-throat profession," he said to me. "Especially when every out-of-work pharmaceutical rep with a low handicap and a contact list of doctors thinks they're the next Butch Harmon."

Whack. The ball soared over the green and continued in the direction of a retention pond. In frustration Paisley Print sent his nine iron helicoptering up the fairway.

"What's with the buggy?" I said.

"DWIs. Technically, I'm not even supposed to drive it on the road, but I have friends on the force. As long as I obey the traffic laws, they leave me alone."

Another shower of balls fell from the sky. *Plop, plop, plop. Splash.*

Two golf carts advanced over the ridge and stopped well short of the creek. Three women got out and waddled off to address their balls. A fourth, who possessed a striking resemblance to Candice Bergen, made a slow three-sixty turn in search of her ball.

Uncle Joe ambled across the bridge and casually dropped a new white ball on the fairway. "You had good distance and the right club," he called to her. "But you lack confidence in your skills. Spend more time visualizing success and don't play down to the ability of your golfing partners. Relax and let the game come to you." He pointed to the new bright-white ball nestled in grass by the creek.

She beamed. "What club would you recommend from here?"

"A putter."

"You sure?"

"The key to your game is risk reduction. See the flag, draw a line, and hit it hard." Uncle Joe returned to his chair.

I dropped down next to him. The damp ground soaked the seat of my jeans. "You were a police officer?"

"Homicide detective with the NYPD."

"And now you hustle customers at a public golf course?"

"Sad, isn't it?"

Candice Bergen waggled her club.

"See the ball going into the cup!" Uncle Joe called. Without looking at me, he added, "That buggy is home. Everything I own is in it."

"But Millie and her mom are rich."

"I came from money, sure. Grew up with my brother at the Canon estate. But when I was around thirteen, I ran away. Joined an Amish community in Mohawk Valley. Moving to a working farm was like going to summer camp."

Thump! Candice Bergen's ball went skipping across the fairway.

"Worm burner," Uncle Joe said to me. "Good one too."

"How'd you end up as a police officer?"

"When I was sixteen, I did what they call my *Rumspringa*. That's like a rite of passage where young people are allowed to see what the rest of the world is like. When my year was up, I joined the merchant navy and became a deck officer. Stayed with that until I was old enough to join the police force. Two months into the job, I shot a kid by mistake. Thought he had a gun. Turned out to be a smartphone. Internal Affairs had to make an example." He stood up. "You said you needed a ride to RIP's?"

"I'm meeting Millie in Rockefeller Park at noon. The two of us are, sort of, looking into what happened to that woman who got killed at the bridge. The person who found the body works at RIP's."

"Ah, interrogations. Boy, does that bring back memories."

From beyond the crest of the hill came a loud *WOO-HOO!* Moments later, Candice Bergen appeared on the edge of the green, arm raised, a white golf ball was in her hand.

"Well, my work is done here. She'll tell the others, and I'll have four, possibly more, new clients. Let's roll."

Half an hour later, Uncle Joe dropped me off in front of RIP's. He had me hold the reigns of his mare while he got Millie's bike from the back of his buggy. "Been thinking about that fellow who you say found the body. Mind if I give you some professional advice?"

"Not at all."

"Get him to talking, then shut up. Once someone starts blabbing, they'll keep at it unless you interrupt. You say he found the body?"

I nodded.

"So right away he's a suspect and knows it. Where'd you say this happened?"

"At a bridge in Rockefeller State Park. Apparently, it's not far from RIP's."

"Know the place. On the Old Croton Trailway. I'm not supposed to take my rig through the park, but sometimes I will. It's sort of a shortcut I use sometimes." He put his hand on my shoulder. "Remember, be firm, act confident and you'll get the truth."

Chapter

10

PRIME-TIME SUSPECT

Here is what I hoped would happen with I got to RIP's. I'd find the person who discovered the body under the bridge on the night Candee Brenneman was killed, ask him a few questions, and leave before anyone recognized me.

That's not what happened.

When Uncle Joe dropped me off at RIP's, the first thing I spied was a Sleepy Hollow Tours shuttle pulling up in the circle in front of the restaurant. The clot of '70s TV Sleuths began filing off. If you know anything about old people—and all them were really old except Charlie's Angels, who were dressed as nuns—you never get between old people and food.

I propped Millie's bike behind some bushes and snuck around the building so no one in the clot would see me. There I waited next to the restaurant's trash dumpsters.

So far the trip had gone better than expected.

I had checked in with Pop and gotten his take on the wolf-man beast of the Bible, learned about the myth of the Wendigo, gotten a firsthand account of the victim from the medical examiner, and made a new friend with a former law enforcement officer. All while riding a train, bike, an Amish buggy, and an old truck. It was like I was in a remake of the National Lampoon film *Vacation*.

There was only one problem. I was on local law enforcement's radar as a possible terrorist suspect, and I had promised Dad I would keep a low profile.

So things weren't all that great.

The bartender, a tall broad-shouldered man, walked out the back door of the restaurant. "Hostess said you needed to speak with me?"

"You found Candee Brenneman's body?" I handed him one of my old business cards.

He frowned at the name on the card. *"Cool Ghoul Gazette?"*

"We cover supernatural and paranormal events. Things not explained by run-of-the-mill science."

Easily six foot three, Mitchell Kraft wore crease-less black slacks, a black long-sleeved collared shirt rolled to the elbows, and black shoes with thick rubber soles. His collar-length hair was slicked back with some kind of greasy gel, a blue and red tattoo above his wrist read MADE IN THE USA. A day's growth of stubble darkened a face so taut that a smile might break it.

He crumpled the card and dropped it at his feet. "Our hostess told me a reporter from the *Post* wanted to chat about Candee. If I'd known it was some scrawny high school kid writing for a blog, I'd have taken my smoke break elsewhere."

I leaned back against the wooden fence, put my hands in my pockets, and hooked one foot over the other. It was a deliberate act of indifference.

Sometimes, nonchalance sells the image, Uncle Joe had advised me on the buggy ride over. *Makes you look confident. Like it makes no difference to you if he talks or not.* But right then, I didn't feel the least bit confident. I felt like a ninth grader hiding out behind trash dumpsters so a bunch of old people pretending to be famous detectives wouldn't turn me into the police is what I felt.

"Why were you walking through Rockefeller Park at that hour of the night?" I asked.

Out came a pack of cigarettes. He removed one and tapped it on the back of his wrist. Tough guy. Muscular guy. He cupped his hands around the flame and lit up.

Through a cloud of smoke, he said, "Couldn't get my bike started that morning. I'd tried jumping it and gave up. It's a quicker walk through the park."

"Your bike, street or dirt?"

"Yamaha YZF-R6."

"Six speed with a multiplate slipper clutch. Zero to sixty in a little over three seconds." I had his attention. "I have friends who ride. Notice anything unusual on your way back that night?"

He took another long draw, paused, and blew rings in my face. "You mean aside from finding a body under that bridge? Nope. Police asked me all this already. In fact, I'm due to speak to a group at lunch about what happened that evening. They're paying ten dollars apiece to hear my account."

The '70s TV Sleuths.

"How much are you paying?" he asked.

Ignoring his question, I said, "The moon that night, was it full?"

He blew a ring of smoke over his head, then nodded.

"So if there'd been another person on the trail, you would have noticed."

"Not a soul."

"Tell me about the body."

He exhaled another plume of smoke in my direction. "I looked over the wall and saw a person down by the creek. That's when I called 911. I didn't know then it was Candee." He flicked ashes onto the pavement. "Look, I get why the cops think I had something to do with her death. I didn't go down there and try to help. I didn't stick around to wait for the cops to show up."

"Why not?"

"Let's just say I had some things on me that wouldn't have looked so good, okay?"

Drugs. Or a gun.

"Plus, to be honest, I thought it was only someone passed out drunk. Kids go to that bridge a lot to drink."

"How long did it take you to walk from here to there?"

"I dunno. Fifteen minutes?"

"The call to 911 came in at ten forty-five that night. If the restaurant closed at ten that evening, why'd it take you so long to call for help?"

He exhaled a curl of smoke out the side of his mouth.

I bet he practiced how to exhale in front of a mirror.

"I didn't leave right away. The morning it happened our manager got a tip that we were getting a surprise visit from the health inspector the next day. They like to make unannounced checkups. You got a dishwasher on the fritz, they fine you like you poisoned the governor. They see so much as one cockroach and they could knock us down to a B rating. That's why we closed early that night. Me and my manager, we stayed to make sure everything was up to code. She left around ten fifteen. I stayed a little longer, then locked up and took off."

"What time was that?"

"Ten thirty."

"You sure?"

"Positive."

"Hey, Mitch," a girl called from the doorway, "your assistant says she can't find the case of Maker's Mark you ordered."

"It's in the supply room."

"She already looked there."

Kraft took another long draw, held it, and dropped the cigarette right next to my crumpled business card. "Man, how I wish they'd stop hiring Barbies with the IQ of a celery stalk. They're nice to look at and all, but boy, are they stupid," he said, as if the girl standing there couldn't hear him insulting her gender. "I'll be right there." He crushed his cigarette with his shoe. "I didn't kill Candee. It's just my bad luck that I found her. The guy you should be talking to is her ex."

"She was married?" I'm pretty sure the shock of that unexpected news ruined the confident image I'd been trying to project.

"To that backpacker who was camping in the park."

"Robert Kincaid?" I said.

"Dude showed up about a month after she died. Came into the restaurant all hot and bothered. Claimed I had been harassing his wife and that's why she was dead. But like I told him, who I date is nobody's business but mine." Kraft leaned close to me and said in a low, hoarse voice, "You looking for someone who might want to hurt Candee, I'd start with him." He wheeled and left.

What a poser, I thought. *What a hothead.*

But was he a killer?

I walked back to the front of the restaurant. That's when I discovered that someone had slashed both tires on Millie's bike. When I looked up, I saw Jessica Fletcher wagging a finger at me through a dining room window.

Chapter

11

THE CRIME SCENE

The arched stone bridge across the Pocantico River had low walls on both sides, waist high. Certainly easy enough to lean over and fall from. Beer cans and cigarette butts lay scattered around nearby tree trunks. Apparently Mitchell Kraft was right; the bridge appeared to be a popular party spot.

When you hear the word *river*, you might picture a wide and deep body of water with maybe houses along the shoreline or, if it's wide enough, marinas. The water beneath the bridge where Candee Brenneman died was a trickle.

Millie was waiting for me in the middle of the bridge with her arms crossed. She had changed into jeans, a lightweight yellow jacket, pink Converse low tops, and a Knicks ball cap—which of course made her look hot in a *Teen Vogue* magazine sort of way.

She smirked. It was not the smirk of someone happy to see me. "You're late," she said. "Is that a thing with you? Being late?"

She seemed to be channeling my mother. Or her mother. I found it annoying.

I looked down, away, anyplace but at her.

"Where's my bike?" she said.

"At RIP's with two flat tires."

Her not-so-happy smirk stretched into a scowl. "Seriously?"

"Both slashed."

"Who would do such a thing?"

"Um, someone with a knife?"

I admit this was not a brilliant answer, but at that particular moment I did not want to get into why the '70s TV Sleuths had made me their Public Enemy Number 1. Or why I thought Jessica Fletcher had cut the tires.

"Have you found anything?"

"Was waiting for you," she said. "I wasn't sure if you had a plan for how you examine a crime scene."

I did not.

But I didn't tell her this.

Instead, I said, "Let's see what we can find."

I should explain that in my mind I had pictured me coming up on the crime scene like you see in TV shows, casually looking around and spotting something professional law enforcement officials had missed. Gum wrapper, cigarette butt, bottle cap with a thumb print on it. You see stuff like this in shows all the time.

Mud and rocks—that's what we found under the bridge.

I dropped to one knee at the base of the stone abutment that arched over the trickle of water. Two months had passed since Candee Brenneman's death. Still, even something as insignificant as branches snapped off, leaves stained with blood, tufts of fur caught in branches, footprints … might hint at what happened that night.

"Did you learn anything from the person who found the body?" Millie said this as if the two of us were working a case on *Law and Order: Teen Sleuths.*

I explained how Kraft had seen the body, called 911, and left.

"So when he was standing up there making that call, the werewolf could have been right here, under this bridge."

"There is no werewolf."

"Well some kind of animal attacked her."

"Brenneman's ex-husband went to see Kraft after it happened," I said, telling her the main thing I had learned that I thought important.

"She was married?"

"To that backpacker. Kincaid."

"And now he's dead," Millie said.

"We don't know that."

"Maybe the bartender killed Kincaid to silence him."

"Or maybe Kincaid was under the bridge when Kraft made the call."

Based on her reaction, I could tell she wasn't impressed with my detecting skills.

I straightened and looked around. "It was a long shot."

"What was?"

"Coming here. Any evidence probably got washed away weeks ago."

"But if you hadn't come and looked, you wouldn't have known it was a waste of time."

Millie was beginning to sound as if she were a private investigator working with her male partner on a cold case—which I found cool in a Pierce Brosnan–Stephanie Zimbalist *Remington Steele* sort of way.

"Hadn't thought about it that way."

We stood there, both of us looking at each other like we weren't sure what to do next.

"So where to now?" Millie asked.

"To see the guy who ID'd the body."

"Why him?"

"Normally they would contact the next of kin. Lacking that, someone close to the victim. Maybe the person she worked for can tell us why Candee Brenneman was on this bridge alone that night."

Chapter

12

FIT TO BE DIED

Inside the GetFit Gym, the stale air had the odor of hot sweat mixed with perfume. Two rows of treadmills faced front windows that looked out onto a busy street. Earbud cords swung as feet pounded moving belts.

"Let me take the lead on this," Millie said. "I don't want you to do or say anything that might come back to Mother."

That right there gives you some idea of what Millie thought of my detecting abilities—and by extension what she thought of me.

"Sure," I said.

Millie approached a man wearing blue shorts over muscular thighs and a white short-sleeved shirt with the words *MARK, ASSISTANT DIRECTOR* stitched above the breast pocket. He stood in front of a long row of workout mats with his hands clasped behind his back. Curly black hair covered his arms, wrists, and legs. His thick neck and shoulders made his head look small.

"We'd like to speak to Butch Prescott," Millie said. "Is he around?"

His wide stance suggested he was there to observe the yoga class, but from the way his gaze fixed on certain more fit women, I had the impression he was observing more than simply their technique.

"Back that way." Blue Shorts nodded in the direction of an area with lots of benches and bars and belts.

The hum of treadmills gave way to grunting and weights clanking.

Butch Prescott was tall, tan, and taut in all the places you'd expect a man who owned a gym might be. He wore black slacks, a blue-striped collared dress shirt, and loafers. No socks.

"Mr. Prescott, do you have a few minutes to talk about Candee Brenneman?"

He studied Millie. "You're Isabel's girl, right?" He said this in a way that made me think he pitied her. "Your mother said you might be stopping by."

"How long did Candee work here?" Millie asked.

"Almost three years."

"Get along with people?"

"Candee? She was as friendly as they come. She took a real interest in our members."

"If the two of you need me," I said gesturing towards a rowing machine, "I'll be over there."

Millie said, "What was Candee's official role?"

"Personal fitness trainer. She also ran our yoga, Pilates, and Zumba classes."

"Had she been having any troubles recently?"

"How do you mean?"

I quickly got into the rhythm. Sit upright, stomach in, shoulders loose. Elbows close to my body with the handles lightly touching my shirt.

"With finances, relationships, that sort of thing," Millie said.

"Not that I know of."

The trick was to keep my shins vertical with no gap between thighs and knees.

"Candee was always upbeat, positive," Prescott said. "It helps to have that attitude when you're a personal trainer. I wish I had ten more like her."

I gradually increased my speed, exhaling on the pull, inhaling on the catch.

"Nick, you think maybe you could stop doing that long enough to join us?"

Crawling off the rowing machine, I said, "Which of the members was Candee seeing?"

"Nick!" Millie arched a perfectly shaped eyebrow.

Prescott frowned so hard the veins in his forehead bulged. "We have a firm policy against that."

"You said she was a people person. Attractive. Fit. I'm sure some of the male members hit on her."

"Nick, stop," Millie pleaded.

"Did you?" I met Prescott's gaze.

"NICK, PLEASE! Tell him you're sorry." Millie turned to Prescott. "He's sorry."

Prescott looked away, took a deep breath, and exhaled slowly, as if trying to regain his composure. "Some of the staff came to me. Said they were bothered by the way Candee favored a few of the male members. If it had turned out to be true, I would have had to fire her. So I rearranged her schedule. The problem went away."

"Was that before or after you two started seeing each other?"

Prescott smiled. It was not a friendly smile. "A long time ago, and I mean a really long time ago, Candee and I went out for drinks at the yacht club. She may have come back to my boat. I honestly don't remember. We both agreed it wasn't a good idea to keep seeing each other."

"Any idea why Candee Brenneman would have been on that bridge at that hour of the night?"

"Take a look around, kid. Do any of my staff look out of shape to you?"

"Um … no."

"And you won't find any either. Staying fit is part of their job. Millie ran that trail almost every night, rain or shine. She'd leave work and run through the park. That was her routine. She carried pepper spray and knew how to handle herself, so I never worried about her safety."

"So if you had wanted to," I said, "you could have left before she did and waited for her on that bridge."

Prescott's expression changed to that of moon-eyed surprise. "You think I had something to do with her death? Wow, did you read that wrong." He untucked his shirt and lifted it. "That scar up the middle of my back?"—he turned around—"It's from where I had two discs fused together. No way I could throw her from that bridge."

"But you could have pushed her over." To Millie I said, "He could have pushed her from the bridge."

Taking me by the elbow, Millie turned me towards the front door. "Thank you for your time, Mr. Prescott. We'll show ourselves out."

On the sidewalk, Millie released her death grip on my elbow. "I told you to let me take the lead. You all but accused Prescott of murder."

"You were being too easy on him."

"But he's a prominent leader in the community."

"Doesn't mean he didn't kill her."

"He knows people," she said. "People like the police chief. You definitely do not want to get on his bad side. You keep acting this way, I won't be able to help you."

"Then don't. I can catch the killer all by myself."

"Okay, now you're just acting like a jerk." For a few moments the two of us stood there, awkwardly staring at each other. Finally she said, "So where to next?"

"Locate Kincaid's campsite. Maybe I'll find some clues there."

"I get finished with piano lessons at four thirty."

"That won't give me much time. It gets dark early."

"Wait for me on the bridge." She placed her hand on my wrist. "Please?"

Even though I knew she still thought I was way outside of her league, I liked the touch of her fingers on my wrist.

"Sure," I said. "But get away sooner if you can. I don't want to spend all night wandering around in those woods during a full moon."

"Because you think there is a werewolf running loose?"

"Because I know there *is not* a werewolf running loose but there may be a killer in the area."

Chapter

13

A "Frosty" Reception

Plates clattered, utensils clinked. The smell of grilled meat and spices came wafting from RIP's kitchen. Jazz music played from recessed speakers set into the wall of the alcove that separated the bar area from the dining room.

Here's what I was hoping would happen. I was hoping I'd walk back to RIP's, get Millie's bike, and—if she was around—ask the manager a few questions about the night Candee Brenneman died. You know, like, follow up to make sure the bartender's story checked out.

That's not what happened.

Millie's bike was gone. So that was bad.

But the '70s TV Sleuths were gone too. So that was good.

I stood in the waiting area while the hostess repositioned a stack of menus. She looked to be in her late twenties with hair the color of pink cotton candy.

Pierced eyebrows, tattoo of a snake on her neck. A nose ring hung almost to her upper lip.

To me, nasal mucus on jewelry is not a good look. But that's just me.

"Will anyone else be joining you?" The hostess asked the question without looking up.

"Your manager around?" I said.

That warranted eye contact. "Is there a problem?"

The problem was Millie's missing bike. And the violent death of a former employee. And a possible murderer working at the restaurant.

"No problem. I just need to see your manager."

From behind, a bow-legged man wearing a brown suit trundled past, his white hair curled tightly over his ears. Leaning on his arm was a short plump woman pulling an oxygen canister on wheels.

"Two?" the hostess said. "Right this way."

The pair followed the hostess into the dining room.

I eased over to the wide doorway that opened into the bar.

Framed photographs of jockeys, thoroughbreds, and horse stables hung on the wall above the gleaming bottle rack. Patrons sat around a long curved counter of dark wood and red leather—laughing, talking, getting a jump on the weekend. Behind the bar stood a tall slender woman with black hair pulled into a ponytail.

No sign of Mitchell Kraft.

"My hostess said you were looking for me?"

I pivoted.

A different woman now stood at the hostess station. She wore black slacks, black flats, and a black blouse with a gold-plated nametag that read *Marilyn*

Frost, Manager. Thick eyebrows. Auburn hair pulled back in a tight bun. She had the taut look of a woman who worked out and enjoyed it.

"I came by earlier and had a chat with your bartender about that night Candee Brenneman died. I thought of a couple more questions."

"Of me?"

"Yes ma'am."

Frost's red lips turned into a half smile. "Please. I'm not that much older than you."

"Sorry. Habit."

"Who are you with, exactly?"

I gave her my business card.

"*Cool Ghoul Gazette?*"

"Brenneman died during a full moon, which I'm sure our readers will find interesting. The *Cool Ghoul* covers paranormal events that can't be explained by science."

"You're not with that group, are you?"

By *that group* I assumed she meant '70s TV Sleuths.

"No ma'am, I'm definitely not part of that group."

"Because I thought they would never leave. They kept stopping the wait staff and asking them about what happened to Candee." Frost motioned toward a pair of glass doors that opened onto the patio, where propane heaters were interspersed among the tables. "Let's talk outside … where it's quieter." She picked a table far away from the lunch crowd.

"Did you know the victim?" I said.

"Candee? Sure. She used to work here. After she quit, she would come in sometimes and sit at the bar until Mitch's shift ended."

"Kraft said the restaurant closed early that evening—that the two of you stayed to get ready for a health inspection. By chance do you remember what time you left?"

Beneath those thick brows, hazel eyes shifted uneasily. She aimed her gaze at the glass-enclosed dining room that extended onto the patio.

I'd read in a review of the restaurant that the expanded dining area at RIP's was designed to give patrons a more open feel. Now I was thinking it might also be a good place for someone to watch us while we talked.

She flipped bangs from her eyes. "We closed at ten that evening. Mitch took off around a quarter after. I stayed a little longer, locked up, then left."

"He claims you left first."

"He's mistaken. Mitch took off before I did, I'm sure of it. I remember locking the door behind him." Frost shifted in her chair, aiming her full focus on me. "You seem awfully young to be going all *Law and Order* on me."

Busted.

Uncle Joe's advice to act calm and confident had worked pretty good with Kraft and (sort of) with Prescott. But RIP's manager sized me up and saw me for exactly who I was—a ninth grader with no business looking into the murder of one of her former employees.

"You a fan of the show?" I asked.

"It got me through undergrad."

I asked, "Have a favorite episode?"

"Um, let me see. Oh, how about the one where a thief breaks into a home, startles the owner, and kills him. Later you learn that the pretty young wife of the dead man was having an affair with her husband's attorney."

"That one was 'Matrimony,' based on Anna Nicole Smith and her marriage to a much older man. In that episode a young gang member breaks into the couple's home. The older husband hears glass shattering, goes for his gun, but is strangled before he can shoot. While the police investigate, the dead man's much younger wife arrives home. You find out later that the wife stands to inherit everything and that she'd been a dancer at a bar where the dead man's lawyer hung out. The wife and lawyer hatched a plan to lure the gang member into the home by promising the teen that no one would be there—which they knew was a lie. They did all this so the young wife could inherit her husband's estate and then marry the lawyer."

Frost eyes went wide. "How could you possibly remember all that?"

"I watch a lot of TV. Too much, actually." I gestured toward the front door. "Couldn't help but notice that sanitation rating is from two years ago."

"Oh that," she said, half laughing. "The inspector we prepped for that evening showed up sick the next morning. He was coughing and sneezing, so I ordered him out. I guess they'll reschedule at some point."

The thought of a sick health inspector wandering through a restaurant spreading germs made me glad I kept hand sanitizer in my pocket. And washed my hands after shaking hands. And—when available—used tissue and paper towels to turn doorknobs in bathrooms.

"Surveillance cameras?" I asked.

"Front door only. We had one on the back near the dumpsters, but someone took a baseball bat to it."

"So no way to corroborate what time Kraft left?"

"I guess you'll just have to take my word." She leaned in, as if sharing a secret. "Mitch didn't kill that woman. He's not like that. He can rub people the wrong way, sure. Customers complain sometimes that he comes off as rude. But in a restaurant, you want someone who senses trouble and knows how to deal with it. I've seen him ease drunks out the side door while at the same time promising them that the next round is on him. He's very good at his job." She stood, indicating our conversation was over.

I remained in my chair. "Any thoughts on who might have attacked Brenneman?"

"Not who, but what. Probably a dog. A big one. We've had a rash of strays running wild lately. There's a leash law, but it's hardly ever enforced."

I stood. "Okay if I stop back later? I might have more questions."

"You say that exactly like that detective on *Men in Blue*."

Smiling, I replied, "Like I said, too much TV."

"Sure, swing back by anytime. I'm almost always here."

As if things were not bad enough already, a West-chester County Police patrol car pulled into the circle of RIP's.

Two deputies got out.

With almost everyone in the restaurant looking out windows, they asked me a few questions, mostly about the bomb I did not have. Then they asked me to take a ride with them.

Which is how I ended up going to jail.

Chapter

14

I Go into the System

Jail isn't some place you want to spend a lot of time if you're a ninth grader. I know on TV they make it seem bad, but a real jail is a lot worse. At least it was for me.

First off, I was terrified. Like, I-wanted-to-cry scared. Like, I almost wet myself when one of the deputies told me they really were taking me to jail.

If you're thinking I'm making this up … if you're thinking that there is no way a kid in ninth grade is going to get picked up and locked up, then you obviously have not been watching the news. Because while boys my age aren't getting arrested in nearly the numbers they used to be, too many of us are still getting picked up.

And a scary thing.

But here's the good news. (Believe me, I was looking for any good news I could find while I sat on a bench waiting to hear my name called.)

The sign in front of the bench where I was waiting to be "processed" read:

"Real" criminals make up a very small percentage of this jail's population. This jail is filled mostly with people who are just stupid, have substance abuse problems, lack impulse control, or are otherwise unable to just stay out of minor trouble. You probably have that one friend who thinks nothing of getting caught driving drunk and then spending a week in the slammer for it. The deputies at this jail know your friend by name. We hope we never get to know you that well.

I was leaning forward with my face in my hands, imagining all the things my parents would say to me once they found out I had been arrested, when an officer barked, "Nick Caden!"

I sat upright.

"Follow me."

Based on how nauseous I felt, I was pretty sure I'd barf on my sneakers before I reached wherever it was we were going.

Officer W. Baxter sat at a desk in a row of desks sandwiched into a large room. An older man, he was heavy around the belly with a broad red face and shiny bald head. He didn't seem excited to see me, but he was polite.

Lots of people were talking loudly—mostly those arrested. But some of the officers were yelling too. The room smelled of BO and burnt coffee.

"Full name?" he asked.

I told him.

"Address?"

"I'm from Kansas, but my family is in the process of moving to Georgia. I don't have a new address."

"Old one will do."

I told him that too.

He put down his pen. "You know why we picked you up?"

"Yes sir … I think."

"We had a complaint that you were carrying a bomb, so earlier today our men served a search warrant at Isabel Canon's home. We looked through your things. No bomb."

I breathed a sigh of relief. Maybe I wasn't going into the slammer after all.

"So why am I here?"

He pulled out a small notebook. "You talk to Butch Prescott this morning?"

"Yes sir."

"Mind telling me why you thought it a good idea to accuse him of murder?"

I gulped. So maybe I *was* going into the slammer after all.

I told him the whole story of how Mrs. Canon sent Dad the clipping of Candee Brenneman's murder and how he'd put me on the train, etc., etc.

"So you're what—one of them bloggers?"

"Something like that, yes."

"You know what we call people like that around here? We call them busybodies, troublemakers, meddlers. Is that what you are, son?"

"No sir, I'm only—"

"Writing a story for a blog, I got it. Except from where I sit, I can't tell the difference between you and those crackpots out there nosing around. I'm sure you know who I'm talking about."

The '70s TV Sleuths. I nodded.

"So I'll tell you same as I told them. We have an open case with an ongoing investigation in progress, and we will arrest and charge anyone we even suspect of interfering with official police business. Am I making myself clear?"

I nodded harder.

"No more interviewing witnesses."

"Got it."

"No more talking to people you might think know something about that poor woman's death."

"Understood."

"And for goodness sake, do not under any circumstances accuse Butch Prescott of murder, again."

"I didn't."

"He thinks you did. Or were about to. Mr. Prescott is a very prominent member of our community. *Very.* He's a well-respected businessman. A member of the chamber of commerce. He's done a lot of good for the troubled youth in our community. A lot of good. Mr. Prescott has many, many influential friends on the force. You understand what I'm saying?"

I nodded so hard I got dizzy.

"Good. Now get out. And don't give my men a reason to pick you up again, because next time our chat won't be this nice."

I wanted to ask if anyone had turned in a pink girl's bike with two slashed tires, but I left without saying another word. I didn't even open my mouth when one of the officers drove me to Rockefeller Park and dropped me off at the trail that led to Robert Kincaid's campsite.

Chapter

15

BAD MOON RISING

A large moon, full and bright, guided us deeper into the woods. Millie walked ahead, leading the way. Every quivering leaf and swaying branch could be mistaken for someone waiting to jump out and grab us. Help was close if we needed it—just beyond the park's boundary. But I hoped we wouldn't.

"If you don't mind me asking," Millie said, "how are we supposed to find this campsite?"

"That's where you and your local knowledge come in."

"But I thought you said you could do this on your own."

"I can. But having help helps. Remember I mentioned that Kraft told me Kincaid came to see him?"

"Yes. So?"

"The article you showed me last night mentioned that he came off the trail near Bear Mountain a month after Brenneman died. He hitched a ride to Peeksville and then a commuter train to here." I paused. "But what if that wasn't the first time he'd visited Sleepy Hollow? Suppose he was here in late September."

"What makes you think he'd do that?"

"A hunch."

"You mean a TV show you watched."

"Same thing sort of happened in *Missing Pearson*."

"You mean missing *person*."

"*Pearson*," I repeated. "It's about a boy named David Pearson who is named after a famous stock car driver. He goes undercover and under the grandstands at NASCAR events to catch the bad guys. He always ends up driving a racecar. Pretty cool show."

"So then the backpacker did what? Killed his ex-wife and got back on the trail?"

"Yes. Then he came off again, confronted the bartender, and … that's as far as I got with my theory."

"Doesn't sound like much of a theory to me," Millie said.

"I admit, it would sound more impressive if I had evidence to back it up, but I've only been here a day."

She sighed. It was not a sigh of confidence for my detecting skills. "Wouldn't there be a record of him making two trips here?"

"Only if he was careless," I said. "Which I doubt he was."

"And if this theory of yours that is not so great is true, who killed the backpacker?"

"No idea. That's why we need to find his campsite."

"In that case, I have a pretty good idea where he camped." Millie pointed up the trail. "If I were going to camp in the park and try to remain out of sight, I'd do it near Raven Rock. It's been years since I've been up there. I used to come with Father. We never camped there but we did picnic. Follow me."

We pushed through a thicket of bramble and thorns, then crossed over a creek. The moon's full-white brilliance should have comforted me, but I had a tingling on the back of my neck that made me wish we had started sooner.

With the light of the full moon, I followed Millie through a maze of branches and heavy brush.

"How good is your werewolf trivia?" I asked.

"Nonexistent."

So I brought her up to speed on werewolf facts. "The first movie to feature a man-turned-wolf was *The Werewolf of London*. The film released in 1935. That was the same year *The Bride of Frankenstein*, *Captain Blood*, and Poe's *The Raven* came out. But it was *The Werewolf of London* that got people all excited. The idea that a man could become cursed and turned into a monster resonated with moviegoers."

We crashed through thickets, then suddenly stopped at the edge of a drop-off overlooking a steep ravine.

"We're not lost, are we?"

Millie gripped low branches for balance and carefully began making her way down the embankment. "Don't think so."

I followed, taking care not to twist an ankle or slip and slide down on my backside.

When we reached the bottom, she pointed up through the trees. "Way up there on that ridge, that's Raven Rock."

I could barely make out what she was pointing at. Then it became clearer. The outcropping of rock had the appearance of a creepy stone castle perched on a bluff.

Cold sweat ran in rivulets down my cheek and neck as we climbed up an embankment. I'm sure some of it was due to the effort of climbing the slope, but most of it was me knowing we were a long way from help.

"In the 'Werewolf of London' movie," I said, "whenever someone mentions the monster, the town's people chant:

'Even a man who is pure in heart,
And says his prayers by night,
May become a wolf when the wolfbane blooms,
And the autumn moon is bright.'

"That's why in almost every werewolf movie there is a wise sage who gives advice to some pour soul living under the 'curse of the wolf.' The sage usually offers some kind of repellent, holy water, or a crucifix. Something that will overcome the curse. It all goes back to that first movie."

"I know I said this earlier, but you're weird, you know that?"

"Weird in a good way or weird in a I-would not-want-to-sit-with-you-at-lunch sort of way?"

"The other."

"Which other? First or second?"

"First."

So I wasn't a total loser. Not that it mattered—she being rich and smart, and me ... not.

We angled through the brush, stepping over the rock-strewn forest floor. High above twisted branches, the moon's face was so bright I could have read by it.

Millie kept looking back at me nervously, making certain I was keeping up. In addition to being smart, rich, and pretty, she apparently was pretty athletic.

After several minutes of walking without talking, she exclaimed, "Ta-da!" She pointed at a jagged out-cropping that towered above us.

The lower half of the rock face had collapsed into rubble. But that wasn't what held my attention. What held my attention was the spindly branches that concealed the small opening at the base of the rocky out-cropping.

I stepped past her, dropped to my knees, and peered in the cave but it was dark out and darker in the cave.

"Could be a wolf den," I said.

"Now you're scaring me."

"If it helps, I'm scaring myself."

"Yeah, that's not helpful at all."

"Want to see what's in there?"

"No," she said.

So of course, that's exactly what we did.

Chapter

16

THE WOLFBANE BLOOMS

"**D**o you have a flashlight app on your phone?" I asked.

"What's wrong with yours?"

"Dead battery. My so-called bedroom doesn't have an outlet."

She pressed her phone into my palm and as she did her thumb lingered on the side of my hand like it did the night before at Cellar 9. I couldn't tell if it was on purpose, but I liked it.

I pushed back branches and waved the phone's spray of light back and forth. Three feet in, the ceiling angled upward and walls expanded outwards to reveal a good-sized cavity reaching back in the rock.

I bent forward and crawled in. "You coming?" I said.

"I'll be the lookout."

"You should see this. It's pretty cool."

"Thanks, I'm good."

Every few moments I paused to sweep the spray of light, revealing damp leaves and small twigs that were strewn about the cave. Feathers and tufts of fur lay farther back in the coolness. The floor, made of jagged stone and gnarled roots, cut into my palms and knees.

You know that feeling you get right before something really bad happens? Like when your teacher tells everyone to put away their books because there is about to be a pop quiz?

That was me—heart pounding under my hoodie, sweat pooling on my upper lip despite the chill in the air.

She eased in on hands and knees just enough to clear the narrow opening of the cave. "What exactly are you looking for?"

"Discarded freeze-dried packaging. Water bottles, caps. propane canister. How much do you know about lycanthrope?"

"Is that a type of surgery?"

"It's the belief that the bite of a wolf can change a person's DNA. The term came about during the time when large wolves roamed Europe. Things got so bad back then that King Louis XV sanctioned wolf hunts. Those hunts are one reason you'll usually see posses in werewolf movies."

"Hey, what's that?"

"What's what?"

"Hand me the phone." I passed it back. She shone its light at a shiny foil pouch wedged under a root.

I pulled it out and read the label. "Mason's Back-country Hearty Beef Stew. Made with real beef sausage and carrots." I tucked it in my back pocket.

"You're not keeping that, are you?" she asked.

"Could have the killer's prints on it."

"How in the world would you ever test?"

"One of the guys in our television detectives group, his mom works at the sheriff's department in Maury County, Tennessee. She runs a detective agency on the side. As long as she doesn't use sheriff's department equipment and works after hours, it's not a thing."

She aimed her phone's light at my backside. "You better check to make sure it's empty. I think I see something moving inside your pocket."

Quickly I pulled it back out and held the pouch at arm's length. There appeared to be a squiggly something inside.

Carefully, I peeked inside, afraid I'd find a worm— or worse.

But the thing inside was not a worm or worse.

"You got any tissues on you?" I asked.

She rooted around in her jacket's side pocket. "It's used."

"That's fine." Using the tissue, I pulled out a thick, green rubber wristband. "I think it's an RFID band."

"An RF what?"

"Radio-frequency identification. A lot of fitness wristbands have RFID built in. That way as soon as you enter a gym, it connects with a hub and uploads your data to a server. Saves members from having to sign in, show ID, and all. I saw members at GetFit Gym wearing bands like this." I dropped the wristband back into the pouch.

CRACKLE!

We both looked up at once. Deeper back in the cave leaves rustled; twigs broke. We were not alone.

"Your light," I whispered.

Millie thumbed off her phone.

Slowly, I backed to where she knelt. Behind us outside clouds swept across the moon, making it even darker in the cave. Directly ahead came scratching, clicking, like claws on rock. My eyes searched blackness; ears strained to detect movement.

Millie eased out of the cave, pushing past the branches covering the entrance. I did the same. An eerie silence reclaimed the forest. The two of us stood at the cave's entrance, listening, watching. Millie's hand found mine and squeezed.

"Let's go," she whispered.

"Fine by me."

We took a step back. Then another. And …

From the cave's blackness a creature flew at us.

Millie screamed and, still holding my hand, pulled us backward and down. We landed in a tangled heap. Its large glossy black shape flew at me; sharp claws slashed at my head. I threw my hand up to ward off the attack, but at the last moment the creature veered away and went winging into the night.

We remained on our backs, breathing heavy.

"Vulture," I said with nervous laughter. "Not a wolf."

Millie raised herself onto one elbow. "Can we *please* go?" She was so close I could smell minted gum on her breath.

Slowly, awkwardly, we untangled our legs. "The pouch," I said, "I dropped it."

"Leave it."

"But it might be evidence."

"And there might be more than a bird in that cave." Millie stood, brushing dirt and leaves from her backside. "Stay if you want, but I'm going back to the place where we veered off the trail. I'll wait for you there." She tromped away, taking her phone. The *crunch* of Millie's footsteps on uneven rocks receded. A deafening silence reclaimed the forest.

I rolled onto hands and knees and pawed around, sweeping fingers across leaves. High above, the moon emerged from the clouds, bathing the clearing in golden light. Finding the wristband may not have seemed like a big deal to Millie, but it was to me. Especially if the data on the chip in the wristband showed her movements the night Brenneman—

CRASH!

I froze.

Directly behind in the forest came the sound of something large and heavy prowling about on wet leaves. I pivoted and strained to see into the blackness. A dark shape moved among trees; branches wiggled ever so slightly. From within shadows came rustling, heavy breathing, like the panting of a huge animal.

Taking cover behind an old log near where Millie and I had landed, I sank to the ground and buried my face in the crook of my arm. *Play dead. The dead are no threat.*

Softly, slowly, the creature approached as if prowling for prey. Its strong musky odor filled my nostrils; a snarl chilled my heart. I flinched at the noise, its sudden and powerful presence looming over me.

I couldn't move, couldn't swallow. My heart slammed against the walls of my chest.

A single drop of warm saliva fell onto my cheek.

"Nick! Are you coming?"

MILLIE!

The ground shook as the creature's massive form whirled and rushed towards the sound of her call. From behind me on the trail came heavy pounding as it charged toward her.

Run, Millie, run!

But I knew she wouldn't. She would wait for me. And by the time she ran, it would be too late.

Chapter

17

Followed by the Moon's Shadow

"Raven Rock in Rockefeller Park." I listened to the battery of questions fired at me by the emergency dispatcher, then replied, "I don't have a callback number. I'm on the shoulder of Saw Mill Parkway borrowing a phone from someone. My name? Why does that matter?"

Vehicles whizzed past. Tires slung melting slush onto my feet.

"Victim's name is Millie Canon . . . That's right, Canon. C-A-N-O-N. Look, can you just get someone up here, fast?"

I killed the call, then leaned into the passenger window to return the phone to the driver. After saying thanks and watching the vehicle drive off, I climbed back over the guard rail separating woods from the highway and retreated through a barrier of trees. Stopping on the paved trailway I looked back the way I'd come. No sign of Millie; no sign of the snarling creature. Clouds swept across the moon; treetops bent. Moonlight painted the corridor with a ghostly light.

I'll be honest: at that moment I had convinced myself that Millie was dead someplace and the creature that attacked her would come back for me, next. I had not seen the animal, but I had heard and smelled it. And if you think I'm overreacting, see if you don't jump and panic the next time a dog sneaks up and growls at you.

"Hey, Nick?"

Speaking of being all jumpy, at the sound of the man's voice I nearly came out of my skin.

"What are you doing out here?" the man asked.

Let's just say at that moment seeing anybody was about the last thing I expected. My heart pounded like a bass drum; knees felt like jelly. Part of it was surprise, but mostly it was fear.

"Uncle Joe?" He stepped from out of the forest blackness.

"My brother's wife called," he said, walking toward me. "How she got my number, I'll never know. I bet I haven't spoken three words to her since brother's funeral. You lost?"

My breaths came in rapid bursts. "Is Millie with you?"

"With her mother," Uncle Joe said. "That's how I knew where to look for you. What are you doing out here?"

"Millie's okay? She's not hurt?"

"Far as I know, she's fine. Why you asking?"

"Never mind. Is your rig close by?"

He pointed over his shoulder. "Back that way."

"Show me."

His buggy was parked in an unkempt area beneath power lines and his horse stood munching on wildflowers. Millie's bike lay in the back, front wheel sticking out—both tires new and filled with air. I had never been so happy to see horse and buggy.

I asked him about the bike.

"Millie texted me to say someone slashed the tires. I figured she would want them fixed," he explained. "So I swung by RIP's and picked it up. Let's roll."

The neat thing about riding with Uncle Joe was that we didn't have to stay on the roads. He took shortcuts, like the dirt service road that ran under the power lines. So even though we rolled along at around ten miles an hour, we still reached Canon Castle only a few minutes after Millie and her mother arrived.

Which I have to say was a huge relief.

That feeling lasted about two seconds.

Chapter

18

FAMILY FEUD

Millie met us in the circular drive. "Mother said for you to park down by the carriage house. You can put your horse in one of the stalls."

Uncle Joe, still holding the reigns, eyed his muddy boots. He seemed to be considering her offer. "Tell your mom thanks, but I need to be on my way."

"Mother insists. She says it's been too long."

"Or not long enough," he muttered.

I could sense his unease. Izzy lived in a mansion, one she'd inherited from his brother. Uncle Joe lived out of an Amish buggy and offered golf lessons at a public course.

"If we all pitch in," Millie offered, "it shouldn't take us too long to get your rig put away."

After we unhooked the carriage, Uncle Joe walked his mare to a stall and filled me in on his day. "I think

I picked up several good clients," he said. "Once the weather turns, people around here hunker down and don't think about golf until next spring. If I can talk people into giving golf lessons as Christmas presents, I'm good until March." He handed me a currycomb brush. "Sadie likes it firm but gentle."

The smell of hay, horses, and leather made the carriage house seem somehow warm and welcoming. I brushed the mare's flank.

"Learn anything interesting about your case?" Uncle Joe said.

I recounted my conversations with Kraft, Prescott, and Frost.

Millie joined us at the stall. "Tell Uncle Joe what you told me while we were walking."

"You mean about what they're doing with DNA and the regeneration of human brain cells?"

"Uncle Joe, you have to hear this. Nick says researchers have started growing human brain tissue and placing it in animals."

Uncle Joe stabbed a clump of hay with a pitchfork. "Can't imagine how that could go wrong," he said, tossing the bail of hay into a stall. "Now do the other, son."

I walked around the mare, started grooming her other side. "First it was only in petri dishes," I began. "But you can only learn so much from a blob of DNA goo in a dish. Now they're testing it on lab rats. Soon they'll be able to grow new cartilage tissue from cDNA. Once they get it perfected, knee and hip replacements may be a thing of the past. Inject new cells and it'll grow new tissue. But that's just the start. Coming up with a way to reverse Alzheimer's and other brain diseases is where the real breakthroughs will come."

Uncle Joe grunted. "Human brains in rats. I know a few ex-cons who I'm pretty sure had rat brains put in their skulls." He locked the stall. "We better head up to the house for your mom has a hissy fit."

Dinner was more health food. I can't even begin to tell you what kind. Weeds, mostly. I drowned mine in raspberry dressing. Uncle Joe shoved sprouts around on his plate as if hunting for a piece of meat.

Millie passed me a dish of pine nuts. "Did you tell Uncle Joe about the wolfdogs?"

I wiped my mouth with a napkin. "In some parts of the country people have started breeding wolves with dogs. Their owners believe if you mix the two, you get a better guard dog. When they're young, training them isn't really an issue. But as soon as they mature, they take on a wolf's aggressive tendencies, making them unpredictable and hard to control. That's when their owners abandon them. Packs have started moving east into larger cities."

Uncle Joe put his fork on his plate, indicating he'd had all the roughage he could eat. "Between smart folks putting human brains in rats and knuckleheads breeding dogs with wolves, I can see why you might think a wolf-thing might have killed that woman."

Mrs. Canon spoke up. "I'm sorry, but all this sounds utterly preposterous to me."

"Mother!"

"Well, it does. Uncle Joe, you consider yourself a free spirit living off the land. Have you ever in your entire life seen a wolf in Sleepy Hollow?"

"Can't say that I have. But that doesn't mean it couldn't happen."

An awkward silence ensued. I still had not mentioned anything to anyone about what I'd heard at the Raven Rock cave. I wondered if I should. It was like Uncle Joe knew something or had seen something and was waiting for me to bring it up.

Instead, he surprised me by saying, "Here's something you might find interesting, Nick. From 1978 to 1982, the US National Library of Medicine the number of crimes reported in three types of towns. Rural, urban, and industrial. I was on the force at the time. We were studying trends in criminal activity in order to make the best use of our resources."

"Was that before or after you started drinking?"

"Honestly, Mother. Could you be any more hateful?"

Uncle Joe and Mrs. Canon locked eyes.

"The report examined acts of violence committed during full moons," he said, turning back to me. "They found that the incidence of crimes increased by a substantial rate."

"Like what's been happening around here," Millie said. It was obvious she was trying to keep peace between her mom and uncle. It didn't seem to be working.

"Well, yes, sort of." He shifted his gaze toward Millie. "Researchers concluded that certain individuals experience what they called 'human tidal waves.' These mood swings lead some people to commit violent acts."

"Sort of like getting drunk and getting into fights at the country club," said Mrs. Canon.

"MOTHER!"

Uncle Joe pushed his chair back and stood. "Better get going. I have a long ride ahead of me."

"To where exactly?" Mrs. Canon's question had a disapproving edge to it—as if someone who lived out of a buggy couldn't possibly be going anyplace important.

"Oh, here and there."

"You could spend the night in the carriage house," Millie offered.

"But dear, your uncle prefers the nomadic lifestyle, isn't that right?"

"Way I live is more of a monetary necessity," he said. "Anyways, I need to be close to the course in the morning. It's not much of a commute from here, but in a buggy on the main highway, I'd be backing up traffic during rush hour." He carried his plate and glass into the kitchen. "I'll show myself out."

Once the front door clicked, Mrs. Canon said to me, "I'm sorry you had to see that. Uncle Joe really has no idea how to behave in the presence of polite company."

"Mother, can we not talk about him behind his back?"

"I would say the same things to his face. Drinking is his excuse for everything. That's why he's broke and homeless and can't find a job."

"He has a job," Millie said. "And he can't help that he's an alcoholic. It's a disease."

"Cancer is a disease. Diabetes is a disease. What he has is a weakness."

"Like you never—"

Shrill, high-pitched neighing stopped Millie mid-sentence. She jumped from the table and bolted for the front door.

I followed, catching up to her in the circular drive-way.

The neighing grew louder, more desperate. Uncle Joe's belongings lay on the ground around the buggy. His bedding tossed, clothes strewn about.

No sign of Uncle Joe.

From inside came the sound of boards splintering, hooves pounding. Splatters of blood, small and dark brown, soaked sawdust.

Millie and I followed the expanding spray of blood to the stall. The mare's front hooves crashed down with a terrifying thud, warning us to keep back. A geyser of hot blood spurted from her left shin, turning the straw in the stall a silky black. Two of the top boards were cracked from where Sadie had kicked at ... something or someone.

I couldn't help but think it was my fault. I had not told anyone about what I had seen or heard at the Raven Rock cave. Now it seemed the creature, whatever it was, had followed me back to the Canons' and attacked Uncle Joe's horse.

From deep in the woods behind the Canon estate came loud gunfire. *BANG!*

Uncle Joe yelled for someone to stop.

Two more shots in quick succession: *BANG! BANG!*

Then silence.

Chapter

19

HOWL OF THE WOLF

"Easy girl, easy. It's okay." Millie spoke in a gentle, soothing voice, hands up, palms out. "You're safe."

Gradually the mare's frantic rearing and pawing subsided.

"I've been robbed!" Mrs. Canon burst into the carriage house. "I've been violated! I'm calling the police!"

"Mother, please don't. That'll only make matters worse."

"I cannot see how. Someone broke into my home."

"We don't know that, Mother. And it's Uncle Joe and his mare we should be worried about."

"Is there a large animal vet you can call?" I asked.

"The police. That's who I'm calling."

"Mother, please. If you do, it's not just the police who will show up. It's the reporters. You don't want to go through that again, do you?"

Mrs. Canon huffed, whirled. "Fine," she said. "I'll call my friend Bonnie at Montgomery Vet." She stormed back up the drive toward the house.

"Think one of us should go see if we can find Uncle Joe?" Millie said.

I didn't dare mention how, only a few minutes after I fled the cave, Uncle Joe found me on the trail. Or how he had mentioned how a full moon caused some individuals to change. Or how he left the dinner table in a hurry. That was my imagination getting the best of me and I knew it.

"After you left the cave at Raven Rock, did you hear anything?" I asked. "See anything strange?"

"Only thing I know is that I yelled for you and you didn't answer, so I texted Mother. She was on her way to meet me. We were going to wait for you, but then she decided to call Uncle Joe and see if he could swing by to check on you. Apparently, it's a thing for him to camp in the park. Why do you ask?"

"No reason." I turned my attention back to the mare. "You better go make sure there is someone coming to take care of Uncle Joe's horse."

As it turned out, I only had to wait about ten minutes for the vet. She arrived in a large black pickup with a trailer attached. Between the two of us, we got the mare loaded.

Standing in the cold moonlight, I composed a text message to a friend from my TVD group. The smell of hay and sawdust and horse hung heavy in the misty air. In the message I requested that my TVD friend ask his mom for background information on Brenneman, Kraft, and Frost. Then I headed up to the house.

As I walked from the foyer past the kitchen, I avoided eye contact with Millie. She and her mom were still arguing about whether Mrs. Canon should call the police. I skulked away to my attic bedroom, where I lay back on my mattress, eyes fixed on the cobwebs knitted between rafters. Sleeping on a mattress on the floor wasn't like a night at the Marriott Courtyard, but to be honest, it was not all that much worse than sleeping on the leaky trawler in Savannah.

My phone chirped.

I expected it to be from my TVD friend.

It was not.

The remains of the victim you asked about are of one Alfonso Gutierrez. Stocky male, five foot five, of Hispanic descent. Cause of death was blood loss due to a torn jugular vein. Gutierrez's last known place of employment was the community college where he'd worked in the maintenance department.

Dr. Sara C. Bisel, MD, Associate Medical Examiner

So the remains of the second victim *were not* Robert Kincaid. Which meant Kincaid remained missing. Possibly alive. Maybe even still in the area.

I texted my friend and told him to add Robert Kincaid to his list of names for background checks.

Chapter

20

BIG REVEAL AT RAVEN ROCK

Millie left a note on the kitchen counter that direct-ed me to a cabinet where I found cereal bowls. She and her mom had left for Millie's tutors.

I poured granola over some yogurt, then opened the email from my TVD buddy. Boy, was there some good information in there. Turns out that Candee Brenneman's death would have solved a lot of Butch Prescott's financial problems.

And Kincaid had previously worked at Westchester Community College in the horticultural science pro-gram. Which meant he possibly knew Pop and Sun Bear. Maybe even the second victim, Gutierrez.

After wolfing down my "healthy breakfast," I went to the carriage house and saw Millie's bike was still there. I guess Millie had picked up Uncle Joe's things and put them back in the buggy, because it looked a lot better than before.

Still no sign of Uncle Joe, though.

After a quick bike ride to the library—where I printed off three copies of the email about Prescott, Frost, and Kincaid—I swung by GetFit Gym.

Blue-Shorts Mark stood near the door, his abs flattened and ribbed under a tight shirt. Tall and broad shouldered, he was just the sort of employee you'd expect to find working at a gym and the perfect representative for GetFit.

Putting on my best smile, I asked Blue Shorts if I could speak to Prescott.

"Saturdays are his days off." Blue Shorts ran his fingers through curly black hair. "Anything I can help you with?"

"Some things came up in his past that I had questions about."

"Such as?"

"It's personal. Any idea where I can find him?"

"At the marina. If it's a nice day like today, that's where he'll be. Sure I can't help? He won't be back until Monday or later."

"Doubt it. I'm trying to get some answers about a woman who worked here."

"The one who died, I know. She was a real piece of work, that one."

I couldn't tell if that was a compliment or criticism. "How will I know which boat is his?"

"The *Fit 2B Untied*. You can't miss it."

Here's what an idiot I am.

After I walked out of GetFit Gym, I thought I'd find Millie's bike where I parked it. I would ride west toward the river until I found the marina where

Prescott's boat was docked. Then I'd ask around until I found Prescott and confronted him about his shady business practices. If he still denied having anything to do with Candee Brenneman's death, I would get the police involved. Obviously Officer Baxter would be upset, but the way I figured it, Prescott would be in a lot more trouble than me. So maybe it wouldn't work.

That's what I thought would happen.

But when I walked outside of GetFit Gym I discovered Millie's bike was gone.

So for the second time in two days, I was the victim of a crime. And I had a pretty good idea who the criminal was: Jessica Fletcher or one of the other '70s TV Sleuths.

Right then my phone chirped. It was a text from Millie.

MILLIE: *where r u?*
ME: *getfitgym y*
MILLIE: *go to here*

There was a link in her message. I clicked on it. A page for the *Daily Crawler* came up on my phone.

WANT TO KNOW WHO IS THE SLEEPY
HOLLOW WEREWOLF?
COME TO THE BRIDGE WHERE THE FIRST
ATTACK HAPPENED
FOR THE **BIG** REVEAL!
TONIGHT AT 8:00 P.M.

A ONCE-IN-A-LIFETIME CHANCE TO SEE THE
WOLFMAN!

AND GET YOUR PICTURE TAKEN WITH
A REAL TV CELEBRITY DETECTIVE

ME: *so?*

MILLIE: *is that your doing?*

ME: *no*

MILLIE: *who then?*

ME: *idiots who keep messing with your bike*

MILLIE: *???*

ME: *its gone*

MILLIE: *WHAT?*

ME: *sorry, gotta go*

I put my phone away. Sometimes it's better to solve the problem and explain later.

Chapter

21

DEAD IN THE WATER

The river was a short bike ride away.

It took longer, walking.

The interior of the Washington Irving Marina ship's store was clean and bright and smelled of expensive varnished wood. There were floor racks of boating merchandise, a display case of navigation equipment, and a wall rack of shirts, caps and foul-weather gear.

An older woman in a maroon sweater was ringing up a customer buying a bag of ice. Gray scarecrow hair stuck out from beneath her faded Washington Irving Marina ball cap. When the woman finished ringing up the customer, I asked where I would find Butch Prescott's boat. She pushed up the frayed bill of her cap, turned to the map of the basin behind the counter, and tapped a red pushpin on B Dock.

A couple of things were on my mind as I walked to Prescott's slip. Finding Millie's bike, sure, but the bigger question was how to figure out who the killer was before 8 p.m. that evening. That was when the '70s TV Sleuths planned to make their big reveal. I didn't have what you'd call a "detailed plan" for identifying the killer: only thing I had was a hunch.

The *Fit 2B Untied* floated between aft and forward pilings, stern to the pier with stern lines crossed and secured to dock cleats. Water hose and power cords lay coiled on the swim platform. I recognized the boat brand—a production motor yacht of the type you see advertised in high-end boating magazines.

Uncle Phil calls that brand a "a floating condo." *Lousy on fuel. Can't back worth a cuss*, he'd told me. *I wouldn't be caught dead offshore in one. But for putzing up and down the Waterway, it's a fine vessel.*

The hose and power cord on the swim platform looked ready to be stowed. Decks were wet from a recent rinsing. Spring lines were coiled and tossed near the anchor well. I had spent almost a month cleaning boats at the Palmetto Island Marina. I could tell when a boat owner was preparing to leave and from the looks of things, Prescott was a man with an exit plan.

I had no plan at all: only a crazy theory I couldn't prove.

I called from the dock, "Butch Prescott?"

Prescott appeared in the companionway, wearing faded red swim trunks and a gray sweatshirt. His face twisted into a scowl. "Oh, please, not you again."

I stood in the bright glare of the morning sun amid boat smells and marina sounds. I had rehearsed what I wanted to say. "When was the last time you saw Brenneman alive?"

Prescott's palms rested on the short fiberglass lip of the companionway threshold. "You sure you want to go there, son? I know Officer Baxter spoke with you. Won't take me but a sec to ring him up, again."

I gulped. "I promise this is the last time I'll bother you about this. And if there's nothing to hide what can it hurt talking to me?"

He came up and onto the swim platform and began stowing the hose and power cord. "Very last time? I guess the day she died. I called the staff together for a meeting. Candee was there. She helped facilitate."

"Is that the meeting where you announced there'd be layoffs?"

"Who told you that?"

"Finances were tight," I said. "You were going to let some staff go. So you wanted Candee there because the staff trusted her, liked her. Knew she would run interference for you."

"I don't know who you've been talking to," Prescott said, "but that's not how it was."

"No?"

"Not even close. We had a meeting, sure, but it was to announce that Candee would be coming on as partner. She'd come into some money and was going to leave and open her own place. I'd convinced her to buy into GetFit."

Prescott had taken the bait—which surprised me.

During our buggy ride back to Canon Castle, Uncle Joe had mentioned how you can get people to open up by simply feeding them facts they know to be wrong. *Some people can't help but point out the mistakes of others*, he'd told me. *Makes them feel superior. And when they do, they'll confirm what you suspect.*

"Where did she get the money?" I asked.

"How should I know? All that matters is that she made a substantial down payment and placed the balance in escrow. Candee had a head on her shoulders. She'd have made her own place work, no question. Ask any of the staff. They'll tell you that's exactly what happened."

Unfazed, I pushed him. "So the deal with Brenneman allowed you to pay off your gambling debt, right?"

"What *are* you talking about?"

"Credit card records show you were in debt deep to an online site called Bet the House. But two days before the staff meeting, you paid your balance and closed your account. I assume that money came from Candee Brenneman."

"Butch, baby, who're you talking to?" a woman called from inside the boat.

He turned back towards the companionway steps. "I need to check on my guest." He disappeared below. A port window in the aft cabin was open partway. From inside came murmuring voices.

I retreated to a dock box to wait and see what would happen next.

I had time. I had a hunch. I also had the feeling that at that very moment Prescott was contacting Officer Baxter. From below came the rumble of an inboard engine; a belch of smoke erupted from beneath the swim platform.

Marilyn Frost climbed up the companionway steps and swung into the helm's seat. "Butch told me what you accused him of. And here I was, thinking you were a sweet young man."

"First impressions can be wrong."

"Yesterday when we talked," I said, "you mentioned that Candee Brenneman worked at RIP's. What you didn't say was that she quit suddenly. Was it because of Kraft? Is he the reason RIP's had to pay out such a large sum of money to her?"

Frost remained calm and composed. "If you are trying to upset me, you'll have to do better than that. Losing your cool in the restaurant business these days can get you fired."

"I'll bet." Seemed like the right thing to say given Prescott's gambling debt. "Here's something else that'll get you fired." I reached into my back pocket. "Being the manager in charge when your company has to pay out in a harassment lawsuit."

"What on earth are you talking about?"

I handed her a copy of the email from my buddy, one I'd printed at the library.

"Nine months ago RIP's settled with an unnamed employee over a harassment claim. Mitchell Kraft was your hire," I continued. "But you couldn't be expected to know everything about every employee. Background checks only turn up so much. But if you'd dug a little deeper, you would have found out that it wasn't the first time Kraft had made advances against a female co-worker. Did Brenneman come to you and ask you to make him stop?"

"No."

"No?"

"Okay, sure, she told me Kraft said some things that left her feeling uncomfortable, but I documented all of it, every word. And to be honest, Candee didn't seem all that upset. I don't think she really minded all that much."

So now my great idea to confront Frost about how her job was a risk due to Kraft's actions didn't sound like such a great idea either. I could see myself being questioned in a courtroom by Frost's attorney and me looking like a complete idiot.

Prescott emerged from below. "Ready to go, babe?"

"Am I ever." Frost relinquished the helm seat to Prescott, then made her way to the bow. With a telescoping boat hook she lifted first one line from a piling then the other.

With one hand on the wheel and the other on the shift lever, Prescott checked boat traffic. "Cast off those stern lines?" he said to me.

I did as ordered.

Frost returned to the back of the boat to gather the lines I'd tossed onto the swim platform. "I never fired Kraft because the police asked that I not," she said, gathering the stern lines. "They didn't want me to do anything that would jeopardize their investigation. I didn't kill Candee. I don't know who did." She pivoted and snapped shut the stern canvas.

Prescott waved goodbye without looking back.

The *Fit 2B Untied* motored out of the slip and into the main channel.

If you are going out for a day on the water, you normally leave the lines on the dock and pilings. Makes it easier to tie up when you return.

Prescott and Frost took theirs. They had no intention of coming back to the Washington Irving Yacht Club. Not for a while, anyway. Which meant my great plan to catch whoever killed Candee Brenneman was dead in the water.

From nearby came the blaring echo of approaching sirens. Moments later two squad cars raced by the yacht club headed south.

I took a final look at the boat motoring away and returned to the marina office. "The *Fit 2B Untied*," I said to the woman in the office, "how often does it go out?"

"Not too often. Why do you ask?

"No reason." The *honk-honk* of another squad car racing past the marina drew my attention. "Sure is a lot of police activity for a Saturday morning."

"There's something going on at the Irving estate." She nodded at the radio units sitting on a shelf behind her. "I monitor VHF and the police frequency."

"By Irving estate you mean at Sunnyside?"

She nodded.

I thanked her and went outside.

The bad news was that Millie's bike had not miraculously appeared.

The good news was that a Sleepy Hollow Tours shuttle had pulled up at that exact moment. The NEXT DESTINATION sign on the front said SUNNYSIDE.

Of course I got on.

Of course I'm also sure I do not need to tell you which tour group was *also* on the bus.

Chapter

22

GRAVE DISCOVERY

"**H**e has a bomb!"

I bet you can guess who made *that* brilliant comment.

"I do not have a bomb," I said to the driver. To prove it, I pulled up my shirt.

"Check his pants!"

The driver waved me on. I guess he'd seen enough teen male backsides in his years as a bus driver.

Jessica Fletcher hissed at me when I squeezed past. No kidding, she really hissed. The '70s TV Sleuths. They had added new members—Jim Rockford, Baretta, Uncle Joe Mannix, Starsky & Hutch, Barnaby Jones, The Mod Squad, Quincy.

When I found a vacant seat (as far away from the group as possible) a woman sitting behind me tapped me on the shoulder. "You with them?"

"No ma'am."

"They say they're here to solve a murder. Our group reads a lot of murder mysteries. *A lot.* I bet if we knew the facts of the case, we could help."

"You should ask one of them about it," I replied.

"I tried. They're pretty tight-lipped."

Looking back now, it may not have been my finest hour, but I told the woman everything about Candee Brenneman's death—including the part where some locals claimed there was a werewolf running around Sleepy Hollow.

She gasped. "Heavens."

"That group is supposed to announce who the werewolf is this evening at the bridge where it happened. You should mention it to them."

This was my way of making sure the '70s TV Sleuths got bombarded with a gazillion questions. Like I said … not my finest hour.

The driver turned on his blinker to pull into the drive leading up to Washington Irving's home. I stood and signaled that I wanted to be let out. He pulled to the curb and opened the door.

Kid you not: Jessica Fletcher booed me as I squeezed past.

When I reached the meadow, I took cover behind a tree, careful to remain out of sight.

A white squad car sat parked in front of the cabin. A pair of officers dressed in black uniforms squatted behind it, guns drawn. Two more officers went jogging around the corner of the house. Still more crouched with guns aimed at front door and windows.

Like before, Sun Bear's truck was parked near the shed.

"YOU, INSIDE," a bullhorn boomed, "COME OUT WITH YOUR HANDS UP."

It was just like you see on TV.

"THIS IS YOUR LAST WARNING."

An officer, squatting low, moved to the front fender of a patrol car. He briefly looked back at his partner, who nodded. Then the officer bolted into the open and ran straight toward and onto the porch. He took up position beside the door.

Sun Bear hadn't seemed like the type to get into trouble. In fact, he struck me as the sort who kept to himself.

Sometimes those are the worst *sorts*.

An officer stepped out the front door and yelled, "ALL CLEAR." Weapons were holstered; officers began milling around.

I hurried across the soggy meadow to see what all the fuss was about.

The officer at the back of the cruiser turned and called to me, "Hey, you! Stop right there." He locked eyes on mine—which when I realized who it was caused my stomach to flip. "What are *you* doing here?" Officer Baxter asked.

"Is Sun Bear in trouble?"

He gave me a quick and narrow look. "Sun Bear?"

"The man who lives in that cabin."

"Didn't I tell you to keep out of this?"

"I stopped by yesterday," I said, "and Sun Bear and me chatted. That was before you and me talked."

One of the officers I'd seen scurry around to the back of the cabin returned. "Sir, we found something in the greenhouse. Better come have a look."

"You." Baxter motioned to me. "Stay put."

"I was in that greenhouse yesterday morning," I told him. "I could probably tell you if anything's out of place."

Baxter studied me. He did not look pleased. "You stay by my side, got it?"

"Yes sir."

The greenhouse looked the same as the day before. In the corner was the large pile of black potting soil I'd seen earlier. Except now a large blue plastic tarp now covered it. The pile of dirt held the attention of all the officers.

"What do we have, here?" Baxter said.

Wearing a latex glove, an officer brushed back dirt. "Nothing good, Chief."

Amid dark dirt a hand poked out. Skin had begun to flake away from a knuckled finger, exposing bone. At the bottom of the pile the front half of a boot stuck out.

Uncle Joe wears boots like that, I thought. *So does Sun Bear.*

Baxter told an officer, "Better get forensics here. No telling what else we'll find." He turned to me. "Things about the way you remember them?"

I looked away and slowly scanned the greenhouse. It took me a moment to get the image of the buried body out of my mind. But after squeezing my eyes shut and opening them, I said, "The pile was here, but there were poinsettias on that table. Two rows of them. They're gone now."

Out came Baxter's little notebook. He made a notation.

"Joe Canon went missing last night," I said. "He's Mrs. Canon's brother-in-law." My gaze returned to the boot buried in the pile. "He used to be in law enforcement."

"Good man," Baxter said. "At one time he was a good officer." He placed his hand on my shoulder, and with enough force to send a message, he turned me around back toward the door of the greenhouse. "Wait by the street, son. That's the best place for you right now."

Chapter

23

CALLED HOME

In front of the drive leading to Sun Bear's a county sheriff's car blocked vehicle access. As drivers slowed, a sheriff's deputy waved them along.

I walked across the street and took a seat on the low stone wall that ran along the sidewalk.

Behind me a man stood in his driveway, shoveling what little snow remained. "Any idea what's going on?"

"They found a body," I said.

"Hotch a mighty, a body. That's something you don't see every day."

"No, I wouldn't think so."

Right then my phone rang. It was Mom.

"Where are you?" she asked, panicky. "Isabel called me. She's been trying to reach you all morning."

"I've had my phone with me the whole time so if she called I would have—"

"Stop talking and listen. Your dad and I will be in Savannah by late tomorrow."

"Tomorrow?"

"I had most everything packed by the time he got here. We're driving straight through, taking turns. I checked, and there's an Amtrak train leaving New York at three. Gets in at around seven tomorrow morning."

"Wait, what? I have to leave today?"

"FRANK, DO YOU HAVE TO DRIVE SO CLOSE?" Mom yelled at Dad.

Which meant she also yelled at me.

I should mention here that my father thinks he is Richard Petty. If you do not know who Richard Petty is, Google him. He's won like a bazillion stock car races, and one time he was ticketed for—this really happened—bump-drafting a slower car in the left lane of Interstate 85 after the driver refused to move out of The King's way. My father loves and drives like Richard Petty even though he never saw him race.

"I'm not even sure I can get to Penn Station by then," I said to Mom.

"Nick, this isn't open for discussion. Isabel said she would be back at her house by two. She'll give you a ride to the train station. Don't make her wait. Isabel hates to wait."

Still waiting for Mom to finish telling me how important it was that I leave right then, I heard a truck horn honk. Mom screamed. Dad said an ugly word. Mom ended the call.

Which turned out to be great timing because right then my phone chirped. A new text from Millie.

MILLIE: *where r u?*
ME: *sunnyside*
MILLIE: *why?*
ME: *they found another body*
MILLIE: *who?*
ME: *don't know*
MILLIE: *mother is upset. police called. they found my bike in a vacant lot. u need to go get it NOW!*
ME: *k*

So now, in addition to getting back to the Canons' fast so I could get my things and catch the train, I had to go by the police station. I walked across the street to the officer directing traffic and asked if he could give me a lift.

He refused.

So that wasn't so great.

Chapter

24
THE FINAL CLUE

The route back to the Canons' from the police station took me near Rockefeller Park.

I need to back up and explain that after the officer refused to give me a ride to the police station he checked with Officer Baxter, who ordered one of the other officers to run me back to the station. Why, I don't know. It could have been that he wanted me as far away from the murder scene at Sun Bear's as possible.

Now this is the cool part.

Since I was riding Millie's pink bike (complete with purple and silver tassels and white wicker basket) through the park on the main trail, I made the decision to swing by Raven Rock.

Turned out Raven Rock wasn't nearly as scary in daylight. I mean, it was still a cave, and caves always have a certain creepy factor, but I wasn't scared. Not like before.

I found what I needed in like, five, minutes.

The pouch of Mason's Backcountry Hearty Beef Stew looked almost exactly like an oak leaf. That's why I hadn't seen it the night before. I slipped it into my back pocket. Next I snapped pics of my shoe prints, Millie's shoe prints, and the large paw prints that gouged the dirt right next to where I had lain. Then I peddled as fast as I could back to the police station.

You might be wondering why I didn't ride straight to the Canons'.

I knew how long it had taken me to ride back to the police station. And I knew, based on how long it had taken Uncle Joe and me to get to the Canons' in his buggy, that I could race back to the police station, wheel around, and race all the way back and make it with four minutes to spare.

But the main reason was that I had checked the pouch. The RFD wristband was still inside. Finding prints on it would confirm my theory of who killed Candee Brenneman and why. I had all the clues, had spoken with all the suspects. I'd even watched the TV episode the killer must have watched.

So I was feeling pretty good about solving the case even if I wasn't going to be around to watch how it ended.

I wheeled up to the Canon Castle with two minutes to spare—and saw Mrs. Canon's car speeding away.

Chapter

25

A Monster Posse!

By some miracle, I caught Mrs. Canon at the next stoplight. A Sleepy Hollow Tours shuttle had broken down in the intersection. Its driver directed traffic onto side streets.

As you probably already guessed, members of the '70s TV Sleuths stood milling around. Pedestrians, and some drivers, stopped to have their picture taken with them. Charlie's Angels had the longest line. Kojak was giving out lollipops to kids. Barnaby Jones held a hand-lettered sign over his head that read

Help catch the Sleepy Hollow Werewolf
Join Us at #BrennemanBridge tonight at 8:00
P.M.

Starsky & Hutch hoisted another sign:

BE PART OF A MONSTER POSSE!

Maxwell Smart, Cagney and Lacey, and Baretta handed out flyers. The Mod Squad posed for pictures with a group of teens. Jessica Fletcher and Jim Rockford stood on the sidewalk with arms crossed, as if disapproving of the whole affair.

McCloud kept trying to herd the group back toward the shuttle, but with so many cast members, the scene looked like something you might see on a back-lot film studio.

I reached Mrs. Canon's silver Mercedes and banged on the trunk to get her attention. She did not look happy to see me. But then again, she seldom did.

We laid Millie's bike on top of my duffle bag and secured the trunk lid with jumper cables. Mrs. Canon's car looked as if it were leaving a yard sale.

I slid into the back seat with Millie. She looked hot, as usual, and smelled nice, also as usual.

"Can't you text your mom and beg her to let you stay another night?" Millie asked. "We're, like, this close to catching the killer." She held her thumb and forefinger an inch apart.

"We?" I buckled my seat belt.

"Who got you in to see the medical examiner? And got you access to the owner of GetFit gym? Whose bike is it in the back of this car?"

I didn't answer. It seemed like the smart move.

Mrs. Canon flipped on her blinker—which was unnecessary, since we were only going, like, five miles an hour—and turned onto a side street.

"Fine. I'll close the case myself." Millie crossed her arms.

I confess: Her willingness to push back was beginning to grow on me.

"No, you won't," I replied. "It's too dangerous."

Millie glanced out her window in the direction of the Sleuths. "Those people out there don't think so."

"This isn't some silly publicity stunt for a bunch of bored tourists playing granny detective. There's a real killer out there."

"So you say. Maybe she wasn't pushed. Maybe that poor woman simply fell from the bridge and broke her neck."

"You heard the ME. There were bite marks on her hands and arms."

"So you *do* think it's a werewolf."

"I didn't say that. I'm only saying it's dangerous to be out tonight. That's all I'm saying."

"What if you're wrong?"

"I'm not."

"But what if?"

I twisted in my seat to face her. "I found the RFD. It was right where I dropped it."

"So?"

"So if a dog or animal or, and I can't believe I'm saying this out loud, a werewolf attacked Candee Brenneman, who took her RFD and put it in that beef stew pouch?"

"What does that matter?"

"It matters big-time. Anyway, it's up to Officer Baxter now to catch the person behind this."

"And I suppose you know who that is?"

"As a matter of fact, I do."

Millie leaned close and whispered, "Tell me."

Our mouths were so close we could have kissed. Not that I was thinking it. Okay, maybe a little. But I knew she definitely was not thinking about kissing me.

"No."

"Because you don't know."

"I know," I said, "but I don't want to accuse someone and then not be around to see how this plays out."

"And then be proven wrong," she said pulling back.

A blaring horn from far away—but not *that* far away—announced the approach of a train.

"Any word from your uncle?" I asked.

"No. I think even Mother is getting a little concerned," Millie replied, quietly. "Not that she would come right out and say it."

Which means the body found in the pile of dirt at Sun Bear's could be, probably is, Uncle Joe's. "Promise me you won't go to that bridge tonight."

"Believe me, I have no intention of leaving the house." Millie winked when she said this—which meant she was definitely planning to leave the house.

"I mean it," I mouthed. "Stay put."

Mrs. Canon glanced in the rearview mirror. "What are you two talking about?"

"Nothing," Millie said.

"It did not sound like nothing."

"Look, we made it," Millie said.

Mrs. Canon aimed her Mercedes into the Tarrytown station parking lot.

"Thanks for the lift, Mrs. Canon," I said, quickly opening my door. "And for letting me stay at your place."

"Give my best to your mother."

"Will do." Before I slammed the door shut I gave Millie one last hard glare. "Promise?"

She winked and said, "Promise."

I hurried inside. Five minutes later I was on a commuter train heading south to Penn Station and home.

Chapter

26

My Trip Home Is Derailed

Four stops before Penn Station, my train pulled up to the platform at University Heights. That's when I got a text.

get off at the next stop!

I stared at the message. It wasn't from a number I recognized.

You know how sometimes you get text messages from people you don't know? Like, they key in the wrong number and start sharing loads of information about themselves (and sometimes pictures)? I figured that's what this was—some kind of fat-thumb-dial texting thing.

ME: *who is this?*

MYSTERY NUMBER: *no time 2 xplane. get off next stop*

In case you're wondering, I had no intentions of getting off at the next stop.

Instead, I rested my head against the window and looked out. To the east, golden sunlight bathed the upper floors of Manhattan's high-rise buildings. Soon a full moon would rise above those luxury penthouses. That was the place to be that evening. Behind locked doors with a security guard in the lobby and security cameras in the hallways. Not standing on a bridge with a bunch of '70s make-believe detectives pretending there was not a real killer on the loose.

The train stopped.

More passengers got on.

The train rolled away.

MYSTERY NUMBER: *i'm not kidding. u need to get off!*

I had to admit, I was a little scared. Here's why. The whole time I had been in Sleepy Hollow someone had been messing with Millie's bike. Which meant they knew my every move. I was pretty sure it was Jessica Fletcher, but what if it wasn't? What if it was Patrick Gabrovski, the man who had tried to drown me? I hadn't exactly done a great job of covering my tracks.

And now the person texting me knew I had not gotten off at the last stop. So I sat there staring at the phone's screen thinking about how, if I was Patrick Gabrovski and wanted to lure a boy like me out of hiding, I would concoct this elaborate werewolf story so the boy would have to get on a train by himself and ride across several states alone. I would isolate him, catch him, and kill him.

If I was a cold-blooded killer that's what I would do.

In a few more stops, we would reach Penn Station. Then I'd have to hurry to the Amtrak ticket counter so I could pick up the ticket Mom bought me.

That's where my focus was when I heard a man's voice.

"You're a hard person to catch, Nick Caden."

I jumped. Kid you not: I actually came out of my seat a little. Because, like I was saying, my mind was on Patrick Gabrovski and for a split-second the man's voice sounded just like his.

Then Uncle Joe leaned over my shoulder and said, "You need to start gathering your things. We're getting off at the next stop."

"I can't. I have to—"

"Be on the three p.m. Amtrak, I know. That's not happening."

The way he said it caused the hair on my neck to stiffen.

Patrick Gabrovski, former law enforcement officer.

Joe Canon, former law enforcement officer.

How did I miss that?

Some days I'm such an idiot.

Chapter

27

Call of the Wolf

We stood on the platform, Uncle Joe and me, waiting for the northbound train to arrive. In front of us the gravel rail bed slanted down into an overgrown drainage ditch. Beyond rusty hurricane fencing stood a few weathered frame houses, close together.

"You seem awful jumpy," Uncle Joe said.

I looked down at the track in front of us and thought: *If I wait until right before the train pulls in, then jump and sprint across, he might not have time to catch me.*

"I should have texted you sooner to let you know I was safe," Uncle Joe said. "Sorry about that."

But if I jump too late or trip I'll be dead. Keep standing here and you'll probably end up dead anyway.

"When I got back to the carriage house last night," Uncle Joe said, "the lights were off and the place locked up. I called, but Sadie didn't respond. On a hunch I texted the only vet I knew." He touched my arm. "You okay, son?"

"It's just my parents. I, ah … got into trouble about a month ago. Did something I shouldn't." From down the tracks a train horn blared—which only caused the uneasy feeling I felt in my stomach to get worse. "I'm still trying to earn back their trust. Me missing the train won't help."

Here's your chance. If you're going to do this, get ready. I casually eased closer to the edge, hoping he wouldn't notice.

"You mean that business in Savannah with your sister?"

He knows. Of course he knows. "You know about that?"

"I've spent the better part of today learning all I can about you." Uncle Joe recited to me my brief history as an amateur detective. "I'm impressed. And I'm not easily impressed. You should consider a career in law enforcement."

"I've been thinking I might check into becoming a forensic scientist."

"You'd be a good one."

Another blast from the train's horn. You know how some people say that when they are in a really stressful situation, they suddenly feel unexpectedly calm? That definitely wasn't what I felt. I felt like I was about to barf.

"You should text your mom. Let her know you're okay."

His comment surprised me. "You sure?"

He gave me a reassuring smile.

"But she'll have a fit when she finds out I'm not at Penn Station," I said.

"Text her."

All my focus was on the rail bed. *Twist an ankle and* …

"Go on," he said.

It's a distraction. The train's horn blared. I quickly pulled my phone and texted Mom. She replied right away.

MOM: *b safe. see you tomorrow evening.*

ME: *u mean morning*

MOM: *evening*□. It's okay, Nick. Finish this thing."

I stared at her text.

"I called your mom earlier to give her a heads-up," Uncle Joe said. "She sounds almost exactly like I remember."

The train barreled into the station, sending a rush of wind at me. My chance was gone.

"You knew Mom?"

"Not well. Saw her at my brother's rehearsal and wedding. A few times after for some get-togethers."

"But how did you get her number?"

The train stopped. Doors opened.

"My brother's wife. She told me she dropped you off at the station. That's how I knew which train you were on. A friend of mine was triangulating your cell and feeding me your location." He paused. "Have you figured out who killed Candee Brenneman?"

"I have a pretty good idea."

"Was it Mitchell Kraft?"

We waited our turn as passengers filed out, then boarded the train.

"He was dating the victim," I said. "He found the body. And he could be the reason for a harassment suit against the restaurant. But he says he is not."

We made our way to two empty seats. I still wasn't one hundred percent sure I wasn't walking into a trap, but there wasn't much I could do about it.

"Anybody else you like for it?" Kid you not: he said it exactly like Frank Cannon would have said it.

"Kraft's manager, Marilyn Frost. She has a different account about who left the restaurant first the night of the murder. She claims Kraft did. He says it was her. The restaurant paid out a large amount to Brenneman. I thought at first RIP's had to settle because of something Kraft did, but he told me Frost bullied Brenneman into quitting."

The train pulled away. Its slow, rocking motion did little to ease my nerves.

"If Frost left first like Kraft claims," I continued, "then she would have had plenty of time to get to the bridge that night and wait for Brenneman. Frost looks like someone who works out. She could easily have pushed Brenneman. I bet she belongs to GetFit Gym."

"She does. I've been doing some checking of my own."

"You have?"

"Once I knew Sadie was in good hands, I grabbed a change of clothes from my storage unit, walked to a truck stop and showered, then caught a ride to the station."

I didn't know what to say to that so I said nothing.

"So we have three people all connected to GetFit Gym," Uncle Joe continued. "Frost, Brenneman, and Prescott. What's Prescott's motive?"

"I would have said it was to solve his money problems. Except once Brenneman bought into GetFit, there wouldn't be any reason to kill her. I think he was counting on Brenneman to help run the place. Maybe run it full-time."

"What makes you say that?"

"The way he and Frost left on his boat this morning. I have a hunch they're not planning on coming back. Like maybe he's retiring. There's also the backpacker. Kraft told me Kincaid came into the restaurant about a month after Brenneman's death. They got into an argument."

"I thought when my niece came by, she said they found his body."

"The remains turned out to be those of a mechanic who worked at the community college."

"So this Kincaid fellow is still alive?"

"I guess. And you know who else worked at the community college?" I paused. "Sun Bear."

"Never met the man, but I've heard he keeps to himself. In my experience those are the ones you have to watch out for. Do you have a plan for what comes next?"

"Me?"

"You seem to know more about this than anybody I've talked with. That includes Baxter."

I gave him a look of surprise.

"Baxter and me go back a ways. He called to let me know you were at Sun Bear's when they found another body."

With that I finally relaxed. No one was out trying to kill me. Patrick Gabrovski had not hired Uncle Joe to kidnap me. As usual I'd let my imagination get the best of me.

"Tell me your plan for catching the killer."

My plan wasn't all that great. But I told him anyway.

"It probably won't work," I said.

"It might."

"And if it doesn't?"

"Let's burn that bridge when we get to it."

Chapter

28

KILL IT BEFORE IT KILLS YOU

My breathing was shallow, ears alert. Eyes searched forest shadows. A slanting shaft of moonlight fell upon the cave's entrance.

I knelt hunched over way in the back of the cave. My scalp kept scraping the low, ragged ceiling. A cool night mist worked its way in and chilled me. A slight breeze bent branches, caused moon shadows to dance.

A wolf can smell blood from a mile away. Blood is its silent call. Was there a wolf in the Rockefeller Park? We would know soon enough.

I cocked my head and listened. Only the sound of my anxious breathing disturbed the silence. I checked my phone. 6:58 p.m. No text from Uncle Joe, no warning of a person or animal approaching.

The cave's darkness felt worse than before, the closeness of the walls suffocating. Part of it was knowing I was alone and trapped—that I was the bait.

Uncle Joe had a good hiding place. From his location he could see the trail from both directions and alert me if a person or animal approached. He was armed. He was trained. But I worried that wouldn't be enough.

Actually, *worried* isn't the right word. I was terrified.

Our plan was simple. Through Millie's social media accounts, we had let it slip that Candee Brenneman's GetFit wristband had been flagged as missing. The GetFit group page was blowing up with people speculating on who might have taken it off her the night she died. I'm not saying it was a great plan. Or even that it made sense. But it was social media, so it didn't have to make sense.

Kraft, Frost, and Prescott seemed like the ones most likely to keep their phones turned on. The odds that Sun Bear or Kincaid would see the post were slim.

Like I said, it wasn't a great plan, but it was all I could come up with.

From beyond the cave came a grunt of effort, followed by panting.

I pressed my back against the wall and braced myself for the shock of company. Still no text from Uncle Joe.

SNAP!

Heart racing, I leaned forward and strained to see past the cave's entrance.

The evening breeze jiggled the spindly vine branches that covered the entrance. The moon's yellowish light on the forest floor. There came a soft sound—the *squash* of paws or feet stepping on wet leaves. Then ...

Beyond the twisted vines covering the cave's entrance, a horrifying creature appeared. Tufted ears sprouted above a knotted brow. Its short muzzle wrinkled back as it sniffed air. Teeth like daggers dripped saliva onto its bristly black fur.

Not a man. Not a wolf either. A man-wolf.

Its shirt and pants were ripped at the seams. The creature stood on two legs the way a man would, but its feet were gnarled, twisted claws that gouged the soft black dirt.

The creature had Uncle Joe by the collar, dragging him.

I held my breath, all hope of escape dying in my heart.

Head sagging, mouth open, Uncle Joe made no effort to move.

The werewolf's claw released Uncle Joe and he hit the ground with a resounding *thump*.

The creature straightened to its full horrifying height and lifted its eyes toward the moon, sniffed night air, and turned toward the cave's entrance as though catching my scent. Eyes stared into the cave. Lips curled into a sneering snarl.

Sun Bear's words came rushing back to me.

You're hunting something that's got animal instincts and the mind of a man. It's as smart as you are. Smarter, actually. Kill it before it kills you.

But I didn't have any way to kill it. Or trap it.

Hellish eyes found mine. A fierce, guttural growl froze me in place. Its wicked claw reached into the cave and hooked Brenneman's green wristband, snatching it away from where I'd placed it.

Suddenly a new faraway sound pierced the night's stillness. Crunch of shoes on the rock-strewn path.

"Nick, I'm waiting. Are you coming?"

MILLIE!

The werewolf turned toward the sound of Millie's voice and sprang into the woods, its blackness vanishing in a blur.

RUN, MILLIE! RUN!

But I knew she would not. She would wait. And by the time she ran, it would be too late.

This time I was sure of it.

Chapter

29

WHO'S AFRAID OF THE BIG BAD WOLF?

I waited until I was absolutely sure the werewolf was gone. Then I crawled out of the Raven Rock cave and made my way toward Uncle Joe. He lay on the ground, still not moving.

"You okay?"

Uncle Joe opened one eye. "Is it gone?"

"Yep."

He rubbed the back of his head. "Not sure what that fool clubbed me with, but he got in a full swing."

"Do you need a doctor?"

"I'll be fine." He pushed himself onto his feet. "We better go check on my niece."

We crept up the trail toward the sound of thrashing and yelling. Millie shrieked, her cries filled with pain and panic.

Rounding a sharp turn, we came upon a small clearing flooded with flashlights. Officers, five of them spaced apart, stood in a circle with weapons aimed at the werewolf. It crouched low and stared around as though overwhelmed by the noise and movement. Millie stood outside the circle behind the officers, hugging herself.

At the sight of Uncle Joe and me the werewolf began snarling and snapping at the officers. Still holding the green wristband, the creature whirled so quick I was certain we'd guessed wrong about its devilish power.

Officer Baxter stood with his palm on the hilt of his weapon, hat bumped back on his head. "I'm tempted to shoot it," he said, "but then the PETA crowd would sue us for killing an endangered something." He said to Uncle Joe, "You might want to check on your niece. She's a little shaken."

Millie leaned against a tree, sobbing.

"Are you okay?" I asked.

She lifted her head and gave me a look that suggested she was glad to see me.

The fact that a loser like me was comforting a pretty girl like Millie must have been a first of some kind. At least it was a first for me. (I didn't actually put my arm around her or anything like that. I wanted to, but it would have felt weird.) Mostly we looked at each other the way kids will when they don't want adults to know what they're thinking.

"Is that blood?" she asked Uncle Joe, breaking our bond of gazing.

He touched the back of his head. "Sorry cuss nearly busted my skull."

"We should probably get you to a hospital," I said.

"My vet friend can stitch me up. I need to swing by and get Sadie anyhow."

There were squeals and shouts as the '70s TV Sleuths arrived, bringing with them a large crowd of curious onlookers. Much of the screeching came from Jessica Fletcher. The sleuths and crowd formed a second perimeter behind the officers.

Officer Baxter took a few steps into the circle. "Hey, Mr. Werewolf. I need you to calm down so I can read you your rights."

The werewolf whirled to face the sheriff, then rose slowly to its full height. Howling, growling, it made a grab for Baxter. Immediately he and two other officers stumbled backward to get out of its range.

"If you don't settle down, I'll tase you!" Baxter said. "It won't kill you, but you'll wish it had."

"He doesn't seem to want to comply," Uncle Joe said. "Mind if we let Nick have a go at him?"

"Me?"

"It was your plan."

"Don't get too close," Baxter warned.

I was scared, sure, but there were lots of police around with guns drawn. And—this is important to know when you are hunting a werewolf—it turns out you can kill a werewolf with a normal bullet. I had checked to make sure.

If Mr. Werewolf decided to go bonkers and attack, there were plenty of other people he could rip apart.

Not that I expected that to happen.

Trembling, I took a few steps toward the werewolf, then stopped, keeping well out of range of his massive arms and sharp claws.

"You're familiar with the headstone in the Sleepy Hollow cemetery," I said in a quivering voice. "The one that reads: 'Here lies Silas Long, half man and half wolf.' You'd have to be a certain age to make the connection. I bet you grew up watching *Scooby-Doo* cartoons."

The werewolf snapped and snarled, but I could tell from the way his shoulders slumped that he understood what I was getting at.

"When Brenneman bought into GetFit Gym, that messed things up for you, didn't it? If anyone was going to be in charge of GetFit, it should have been you. Maybe you only meant to threaten her, convince her to back out of the deal. So you waited on the bridge that night, and when Brenneman jogged by, you confronted her over it. Was her fall an accident?"

He lifted his head high and howled.

I said to Officer Baxter, "Should you read him his rights?"

"Why? Right now all we have is a citizen having a conversation with a werewolf."

"After you killed her," I continued, "you ripped her throat apart and planted wolf-like prints around the body. I guess that was to make it appear that an actual wolf or dog was attacking people."

The werewolf snarled.

All in all it was quite impressive. Almost believable.

"If I had not found the GetFit wristband, I might never have made the connection."

The werewolf grew still, dropped his head, and stared at the ground.

"There were only two people in Rockefeller Park that evening wearing GetFit wristbands. Candee

Brenneman and you. The tracking data on the Get-Fit server proves it. And Officer Baxter confirmed this evening that your prints are on Brenneman's wristband. What I don't get is why you didn't simply throw hers in the garbage. Or creek. Why try to hide Brenneman's RFD wristband in the beef stew pouch in the cave?"

The werewolf roared with less enthusiasm than before. This time it was the snarling sigh of a man. Slowly, the werewolf clamped its claws on the sides of its head and pulled upward. The hair and mask came off.

Blue-Shorts Mark glared at me. "Stupid kid. Why couldn't you mind your own business?" He turned to Officer Baxter. "I want a lawyer."

"Smart move," Baxter said. "Cuff him."

"You didn't answer his question," said Frank Cannon. "Why did you hide the victim's GetFit wristband in the cave? That was dumb."

"And stupid," said Maxwell Smart. "Especially if your prints were all over it."

Kojak shook his head. "You're an insult to the intelligence of criminals everywhere."

The remainder of the '70s TV Sleuths berated Blue Shorts while an officer handcuffed him. The onlookers clapped. In a way, I sort of felt sorry for Prescott's assistant. But not too sorry. After all, he had killed Candee Brenneman. And maybe two others.

By the time Officer Baxter officially read Blue-Shorts Mark his rights, news crews had begun to arrive—alerted, no doubt, by the Sleuths. That was my cue to disappear. I melted into the woods.

Chapter

30

FISHING FOR ANSWERS

Three days after I returned home to Savannah, Georgia, from Sleepy Hollow, Dad announced the two of us were going fishing.

After promising Mom we would be back before lunch, Dad and me rode to Tybee Island. A tanned and bearded fishing guide met us at the marina. The mist had begun to burn off, leaving a clear and cloudless morning. From the east a breeze carried the salty smell of the Atlantic and the promise of a warm afternoon.

Dad and I got into the rental and lathered our faces, necks, backs of our hands with SPF 50 sunscreen. We wore lightweight long-sleeved shirts, long pants, socks and waterproof boat shoes, and wide-brim straw hats. Mom had warned that with our pasty-white winter skin, we'd burn in a skinny minute. She'd insisted we put on sunscreen. Me especially.

The guide headed straight for Cock Spur Island Channel, zipping across glassy shallows flanked by mud flats and sandy shoals. He told Dad the tide was perfect for red drum and speckled trout. "If you don't have fish for lunch, you're simply not trying," he'd told Dad.

When we got to Lazaretto Creek, our guide dropped the anchor and backed down to make sure it set. Then he radioed the marina. A few minutes later an inflatable arrived. Our guide crawled in the marina's tender, wishing us luck. Dad and me knew the way back, had charts, cell phones, and the VHF radio. There was almost zero chance we'd get lost.

Which of course is exactly what did.

"We're lost," Dad said.

"I was going to say something earlier, but you seemed pretty sure we were in the right channel."

"We're not."

"So turn around and head back."

"I would except ..." Dad pointed way out behind us at the wide bay we'd just crossed.

It took me a second to see the problem. Then I noticed a smear of white foam spreading across brown water.

"Tide's running out," he said. "We go back the way we came, we'll get stuck for sure."

"So what now?" I asked.

Dad opened his tackle box and rooted around until he found the lure he was looking for. "We fish."

I can't remember if I mentioned this or not, but Dad isn't the sort to get too excited about stuff. I mean when I mess up, sure, but not other things. Like getting stuck on the water without any way back to land, that might bother some people. Mom would freak. My sister too.

But to Dad it was an adventure.

To be honest, I think he was just happy to be in a boat fishing in late November.

"How's Pop?" he asked.

"He didn't recognize me at first. I left thinking that we should all go visit him soon."

"Your mother would like that."

I couldn't help but think that Dad might enjoy visiting, too. It would give him a chance to see Mrs. Canon, again.

He held a lure and hook out to me. "You know how to thread a line?"

"Maybe you can do the first one."

Dad went to work preparing my rig. "How did you know who the killer was?"

"I didn't. Not at first. I only had a hunch."

"What tipped you off?" He doubled the loop back, leaving a loop large enough to pass the hook or lure through.

"The way he looked at the women in the yoga class. He worked at a gym. It's sort of like the one near your real estate office, only larger. It seemed like he was working there for the wrong reasons."

"There was a guy like that back at the plant. Women kept complaining he was looking down their shirts. He eventually got fired."

"I didn't think any more about it until later when I found the victim's wristband hidden in that cave. The connection to the gym reminded me of a show I'd watched on the train ride up."

Dad sent his hook and lure zinging. It splashed and he took in the slack. After casting several times, I finally landed my lure in the middle of current running behind the boat. "It always comes back to those shows, doesn't it?" he said.

"Thing is, Dad, it works. Like in this case the killer actually used a stunt from an old *Scooby-Doo* episode called, *Who's Afraid of the Big Bad Werewolf.* Millie actually tipped me off to that one."

"So Mrs. Canon's daughter helped."

"Big-time."

"You say that like you two hit it off?"

"She's fun. And pretty. And smart."

"Sounds like her mom."

I didn't mention to Dad that I wasn't a fan of Mrs. Canon—that I thought she acted spoiled and mean to Uncle Joe.

The skiff was anchored up current of the bridge. With water boiling around the shallows, first one fish, then another, began testing the bait. I studied Dad. He was the fisherman in the family. At least he'd certainly done more fishing than I had.

"When you set the hook, don't snap or jerk too hard," Dad said. "Else you'll pull it through its mouth. A short, quick tug should be enough." His eyes remained fixed on his rig's taut monofilament line. "How come those two people who worked at the restaurant had differing accounts about who left when?"

"That stumped me until I saw Frost and Prescott motor away on his yacht. Then it made sense. You can sort of understand, right?"

Dad tore his gaze away from his line and eyed me. "How so?"

"This. Us. Getting away on a boat. Frost cost the owners of the restaurant a lot of money. If it wasn't for the timing, they'd have fired her on the spot, but summer in the Adirondacks is a busy time. They had to wait until the end of the season to get the person they wanted to replace her. Millie's uncle told me that in a text yesterday."

"But why lie about what time she left?"

"Because if word got out that the manager of RIP's was dating the owner of a health club where a former RIP's employee recently purchased part ownership, the owners might accuse her and Prescott of 'colluding to defraud.' She left before Kraft that evening so she could meet Prescott and make plans for getting away. There never was a health inspection scheduled."

The line oscillated on the water. I kept my thumb on the reel, drag set loose, but not so loose it would backlash.

"After talking it over with Millie's uncle," I said, "we both agreed that the owners of RIP's will probably come after Frost and Prescott. It's because of Frost that Candee Brenneman walked away with all that money from the harassment suit. And that money went straight into Prescott's pockets. If they can implicate Prescott in the scheme, they may try to take his yacht and any other assets he may have."

"Implicate?"

"Dad, I watch cop shows, remember?"

"As if I could forget." He reeled in and cast closer to the bridge. "So it's possible the restaurant owners will end up owning GetFit."

"I suppose."

There was a slight tug on my line. Hardly notice-able. I removed all slack in the line and stopped. Very slowly I lowered the rod until it was pointing at the spot where my lure had gone in.

The tugging returned. I waited, felt the fish hit, and immediately snatched my rod up and back. Instantly the line sliced sideways across the water.

"Good job, buddy. Now work him back towards the boat." Dad reached behind me to get the net and got ready to scoop in the fish. "What about the guy you went to see about that Wendigo creature? The one with the greenhouse?"

"According to Uncle Joe, Sun Bear was on the Washington Irving estate putting out poinsettias the entire time Officer Baxter and his men were at his cab-in."

"Have they confirmed the body in the pile of dirt was Kincaid's?"

"Actually, no. The hand belonged to the dead me-chanic, Gutierrez. Boot too. The ME could have told me this in the text she sent me, but I guess she didn't think it was important. Blue Shorts was trying to throw suspicion on Sun Bear."

Dad leaned over the side of the skiff with the net. "Keep him away from the outboard. Don't want to get the line tangled in the prop."

I reeled the fish in closer toward the side of the boat, Dad scooped, and we had ourselves a dark-red-dish fish.

"Red drum," he said.

"How can you tell?"

"That eyespot near the tail. Good size too. It'll grill up nice." Dad dropped my catch into the cooler. "So the backpacker is alive?"

"I guess. In his text Millie's uncle said he thinks someone spotted Kincaid a little south and west of Mount Katahdin in Maine. That's near the end of the Appalachian Trail."

"Seems odd that Prescott's assistant would kill someone just so he could end up working longer hours."

"He was a star quarterback in high school," I said. "Played backup in college. I guess he felt his talents weren't fully appreciated at GetFit Gym. When Prescott sold Brenneman half ownership, he probably sensed his days were numbered. There had already been several complaints by women members. I doubt Candee Brenneman would have put up with that."

"So really, there is just the one murder, plus the maintenance guy."

"Right."

"Any idea how the Brenneman woman ended up mauled? Or how those paw prints ended up around her body?"

"No idea, Dad."

"And the guy who pushed her, the one who dressed up like the Wolfman, he swears he didn't touch the victim except to take her wristband?"

I nodded. "Makes sense, actually. The ME has already confirmed Brenneman died of blood loss, not from the broken neck. That's a lesser charge."

Dad said, "Why risk going down there to get the wristband at all? Why not simply run?"

"He knew if he put the wristband in the cave then it wouldn't be able to signal its location. Rock is dense. That part was pretty smart. Leaving his prints, not so much."

"You realize there's a problem."

"If Blue-Shorts didn't rent the Wolfman outfit until the day he was caught and he's telling the truth about not having a dog with him that night on the bridge, then what attacked Candee Brenneman while she lay there with a broken neck? To be honest, Dad, I have no idea. That part has me stumped."

"But you're sure it wasn't werewolf."

"I'm sure, Dad. There's no such thing."

The End ...

... OF ME

On the last day of the year a plain brown package addressed to Nick Caden of Kansas arrived at our new apartment. Inside the package was a book: *Me Speak Gullah!* by Jane Jenkins. An unsigned note said, "Wish I could get home for Christmas break, but some of the girls and me are going snowboarding in West Virginia. Maybe after the first of the year I'll get back for a few. Meantime, learn to speak local, Kansas." The book and note from Kat put a smile on my face.

I miss that girl. Can't explain why. We'd only spent a couple weeks together. But I could not stop thinking about her.

Mom and Dad, Wendy and me were on the small balcony of our tiny apartment. I could go on and on about how compact our unit was, or how I had elected to sleep on the couch each night rather than in a room with my sister. The important thing to know is that we were all outside on our apartment balcony on the last day of December. Had I still been living in Kansas I would have probably been shoveling snow.

Mom was going through a stack of bills and credit card statements. Wendy wanted all of us to stop what we were doing and listen while she told us all about an invitation she'd received to a cheerleading camp in Charleston that *only* costs two thousand dollars. Dad chuckled, but not sarcastically and not at my sister's news. He was reading a letter addressed to him—which was odd, since Dad never gets mail.

"You gotta read this," he said, handing me the letter. "This guy's a riot."

Dear Mr Caden;

Thank you for your recent inquiry as to the availability of the Fit 2B Untied. I'll be honest: I had no idea anyone would ever be interested in this boat. Especially in this economy. But knowing how a man in your position would hate to pass up a good deal, I charged ahead and drafted your checking account the full asking price for this perfect yacht. I'm enclosing a picture. As you can see, she's a classic. Or was. (More on this, later.)

I originally thought $39,000 sounded a little high for a 27-foot boat in this condition, but the man at the salvage yard assured me that was a fair price. The fact they don't make this model any more concerned me at first. I thought maybe the design had fallen out of favor, but my contact explained that it had something to do with lawsuits and actuaries. Anyway, when I heard that, I began to feel better.

Now, knowing how men like you like to have things done right, you'll be interested in the information I managed to gather about the engine.

First, you'll be pleased to know we were able to knock the rust off the engine block and find the serial number. We traced it back and found that it **WAS NOT** originally a diesel engine. I must say I was surprised. It sure smelled and leaked oil like a diesel engine. My contact at the salvage yard said the engine could probably be converted back to gasoline, if you like, making it as good as new. Knowing how important it is to move fast with these projects, I went ahead and drafted your account the $8900 fee so the men on the yard could get started.

I looked up at Dad. "Is this a joke? Did this guy really steal money from us?"

"Who stole money?" Mom asked.

"No one stole any money," said Dad.

"Can I go?" Wendy asked for, like, the hundredth time. "Pretty, pretty, please?"

My parents continued ignoring my sister.

"Let me see that," Mom said, reaching for the letter.

"Sylvia, really, it's nothing. Someone is having a little fun with me and Nick, is all. Let him finish, then you can read it."

Wendy, still pleading: "Can I just this once?"

"No," Mom said.

"We'll see," said Dad.

About the boat itself. Who would have thought that for that price it would have a big hole in it?

It sure caught me by surprise, I'll tell you that. I didn't even notice how low she rode in the water until we did the sea trial. The two of us barely escaped before she sank. While swimming back to the dock I kept saying to the salvage yard owner "Boy, won't Mr. Caden be surprised."

By the way, after the sea trial the man working on the engine restoration project must have gotten sick or something because I haven't seen him since I gave him the money I drafted out of your account.

Oh, here's some more good news. I ran into an engineer from the Ukraine who said he could refit your boat for $22,500. He said he used to work for the Russian navy before he retired to the States. His last retrofit was that submarine, the Kursk. That's the one that blew up and sank. But Uri—that's his name—said he stands behind his work. "Way behind," I think were his exact words.

I drafted your account for half the renovation fee because I knew, based on the sparse amenities on your yacht before it sank, that you'd want any improvements done before you saw it. I'm sure Uri is down there in the water right now looking for your boat because I haven't seen him since.

One final thing.

The salvage yard owner threw in a 5-gallon bucket of something called "boat rot" that he said would come in handy. I thought it tasted a little like Nescafé coffee but a guy down at the ship's store said it made wood much stronger and that all wooden boats, especially one's as old as yours, kept buckets of this stuff aboard.

P.S. There is an alternative to raising your boat if we can ever find it. There is a gal down here in Nassau who offered to give your entire family scuba lessons for the low price of just $7,500. If you went that route you, your wife, Wendy, and Nick could enjoy your new boat right where it is. Of course, you wouldn't be seen by as many of your friends, so that's something to keep in mind. I wanted to keep your options open, so I drafted another $3000 from your account for the scuba class.

If I can be of any further help, call Pat at Pat's Pub on Paradise Island. I won't be here, but you can leave a message. And don't worry about calling collect. I went ahead and drafted a couple hundred dollars from your account to cover the phone calls. You can thank me later.

P.S.S. Tell Nick they found the creature that killed those two people in Sleepy Hollow.

I'm a big fan of your boy. Have been since he began writing for the Cool Ghoul Gazette. The Westchester County Coroner said it was a wolfdog that killed both of them. "This creature is basically a wild animal in a dog's body," she told me. I must say, two deaths from a wolfdog in two months sounds like something Officer Baxter should be looking into. Well, that and the vandalism and theft of a girl's pink bike.

But from what I can gather, now that they have charged that fellow at the gym with that woman's death, Baxter and his men are not overly concerned. Law enforcement can lose focus that way, sometimes.

You and your family take care, Mr. Caden. Hope to see you soon.

Signed: Pat. G.

I looked up at Dad. He still wore a half-smile. "You know who this is, right?"

"Have no idea, buddy, but I'm tempted to call him at that bar to see if he answers."

Mom snatched the letter from me.

"It's him," I said to my parents. "It's Patrick Gabrovski. He knows I'm alive." I took a deep breath. "And he's coming for me."

The worst kind of monster is the one you never saw coming.